CIRCA 2047

THE ORBIT OF DOOM

AF646858

IMA ASTRONYM

First Edition: December 2025
Printed in India

Printed at: EPG, Bengaluru
Typeset in Adobe Garamond Pro

ISBN: 978-93-5592-384-4

Cover Design: Ima Astronym

Publisher: Ima Astronym
Lalbagh Road Cross,
Bengaluru - 560027

Web: https://imaastronym.com/
Email: imaastronym@gmail.com
Instagram: @imaastronym
Facebook: /ima-astronym
Twitter (X): @imaastronym
YouTube: /imaastronym
LinkedIn: /imaastronym

Dedication

To the Good of Humanity

Acknowledgment

My sincere thanks to one & all, known & unknown for their kind support & good wishes.

Introduction

What begins as an obscure scientific expedition by a team of seekers—scientists, explorers, skeptics—thrust into the unknown, their discovery is more than an island lost to maps with secrets buried under the sands of time & memories long forgotten.

The small & insignificant looking kabbot becomes the cause of a consequential future altering the course of the collective destiny of planet Earth.

The interplay results in Earth being held hostage by a never-heard, never-seen-before hostile alien force—one belonging to a civilization so advanced, it makes our existence seem primitive.

Is there anyone who can develop a counter to this threat?

Is there anyone who can save humanity from the clutches of the aliens?

And the biggest question: Will Earth survive, or Will Earth succumb?

Welcome, join the mission & make your impact on the destiny of Humanity.

Contents

Chapter 1

Expedition MESPA

(Mapping of Exotic Species of Plants and Animals)

The sun slowly rose over the horizon, coloring the sky with shades of amber and pink. The air was cool and the water sparkled under the beautiful sky. The wave restless in it's too and fro motion brought with it pretty looking shells and leaving them abandoned on the shore. For the fisherman, this was a usual sight and had lived through the view innumerable times.

Aboard his small wooden boat, the fisherman stood as a silhouette against the horizon, his figure rugged and timeworn. His hands, roughened by years of labor, gripped the edge of the vessel as he leaned over to check his nets. Each line and crease on his face told a story of his persistent behaviour, of braving storms and endless days under the sun. The salt from the sea and the wind had carved into him an endurance, blending his essence with that of the ocean he knew so well.

The morning air was mixed with the saltiness of the sea and the fishy aroma. His net was heavy, glistened with seawater and varied writhing fish hoisted in the air with wet fins flapping. To him it was just another day with a bunch of gain from his lot at least that's what he thought until something caught his eye.

Between the silver scales and slapping tails was a peculiar object. The object almost felt alive, something about it was just different. He separated the object from the lot of fish he had collected from the sea. At first he hesitated to take the object in his hand. But after contemplating for about 2 minutes, he picked up the shiny silvery metallic object and ran his fingers over the smooth surface of the peculiar object; it had a grooved, spiral pattern on the inside. Since it was a metallic object, the sun reflected on its surface making it seem like a beautiful rainbow coloured body.

But after years of working at the sea and finding some junk almost everyday made his curiosity wash away. It made him think as if that object was just another piece of trash that the tourist must have thrown in the sea. The sea was no stranger to the garbage and broken shells that were thrown and found by the fishermen. The fisherman tossed the object in the nearby pile of trash that he had created to separate the fish from the trash. Soon after the fisherman got busy with his routine and the object was forgotten.

As his work for the day came to an end, his eyes lay fixed on the pile of trash and the shiny silvery object. He felt uneasy looking at it, but yet shrugged that feeling off. Picking it up, he placed the object in his pocket, keeping it safe.

"Would that be valuable?" he thought. If he kept it as a relic, it would be of no use and thus thought of selling it off and earning some money out of it. His walk to the market felt seemingly longer than usual. His mind had various thoughts as to how did this object reach the sea, was that from some wrecked sunken ship, was that even worth a penny or was it worth in thousands and out of all the questions that lingered in his mind the biggest one was would it be useful for him to keep the object.

The fisherman was quick at decision making since that was his strength and something on which his life depended on. This object, however, defied his intuition. Its material felt too refined for anything mundane, its surface was too pristine to belong to the chaos of the sea. There was something else too- an almost imperceptible hum that seemed to emanate from the object. It was so faint that he wondered if he was imagining it. The sensation wasn't sound, exactly but a vibration, a whisper of energy that tickled the edge of his awareness.

Something about the object demanded attention, though he couldn't say why. It was as if it carried with it a presence- a quiet but undeniable assertion that it did not belong here, yet it had arrived for a purpose. The fisherman shook his head, trying to dispel the unease creeping into his thoughts. He was a man of the sea, grounded in the tangible and the immediate. Mysteries and speculations had no place in his world.

The object in his bag seemed absolutely strange. A day that began with the regular hustle and bustle was actually just the peace before the coming of a storm. The fisherman was absolutely unaware of what was going to happen.

★★

The fisherman neared the market with his collection and the strange object in his pocket and made his way towards the antique shop. This was a place where livelihood thrived. The market place was filled with a colourful sight, with the fresh smells of flowers and various food items, and the sound of the buzzing market. Vendors shouting to sell their goods, their voices rising with the bargaining buyers.

The air was thick with the scent of flowers, vegetables, and food with a mix of aromatic spices. Curry powders, cinnamon sticks and dried chillies lay in neat piles, their bold colours a beautiful contrast to the silver fish.

Deep in the market was the antique shop. The shop was a peculiar place filled with antiques and curiosities from far-off lands. The shopfront was narrow and unassuming, its dusty windows obscured by a cluttered display of peculiar artifacts: porcelain teapots, rusted ship compasses, and gilded picture frames with peeling gold leaf. A lone brass bell hung above the door, chiming softly whenever a visitor entered.

He entered the dimly lit shop, "Time Machine" and was greeted with the scent of incense. The shop was a labyrinth of shelves, each one groaning under the weight of treasures and trinkets. It was filled with the scent of old paper, varnished wood, and a faint trace of incense that seemed to linger perpetually. The shop's layout was chaotic but deliberate, as though the owner, despite the disorder, knew exactly where everything was. A globe with chipped paint stood in one corner, delicate figurines, tarnished silver goblets, and stacks of leather-bound books with titles in languages long forgotten. There were jars filled with sand from distant beaches, pressed flowers encased in glass, and peculiar objects whose purpose was unclear—an ivory carving shaped like a dragon's tooth, a telescope missing its lens, and a bundle of faded letters tied with twine.

The counter was at the end of the shop, and behind it stood an old Chinese man, the owner of the shop. On top of the counter hung a signboard which said "Every piece has a story". The old Chinese man looked up, his face a roadmap of wrinkles. His single broken tooth was noticeable as he smiled; a crooked, almost mischievous grin. His voice, when he spoke, was deep and gravelly, like stones scraping against each other.

"What've you got for me today?" he asked, his eyes scanning sharply and calculative as they flicked up from the ledger he had been studying before looking back.

The fisherman, hesitant at first, felt the presence of the object in his pocket before pulling it out. At first he thought the object held some value but looking around the shop he realized it was of no importance and was just some other less extraordinary object retrieved from the sea.

He pulled out the metallic silver object and placed it on the table. "Found this in my net this morning. Looks rare, doesn't it? Maybe something valuable?" His voice held a hopeful edge. The old man picked it up, turning it in his fingers. His eyes gleamed momentarily before he scoffed. He picked it up, his gnarled fingers turning it over with a practiced ease that suggested years of handling the bizarre. The metallic surface caught the dim light of the shop and shimmered faintly under it.

The silence was longer than what the fisherman had imagined. He once again repeated, "What do you think, how important is it?"

"Worth a few pennies, nothing more," the shopkeeper replied.

"How come no more? It looks valuable."

"It's just a piece of metal. Nothing unique or valuable. I don't think a piece of scrap would be worth more than a few pennies."

"It does not look like scrap considering its metal, sheen and weight as well."

"Either take it or leave it," his tone wavered a little.

Hesitantly the fisherman agreed to the bargain since he had nothing to do with that invaluable piece of metal. He looked defeated as he turned to leave the shop disappointed. He thought it would have been better to leave the object with the rest of the trash instead of bringing it there just for a few pennies.

The transaction was completed and the object was placed on one of the similar looking shelves. Beside it lay an old compass, small glass bottles with some liquids and a collection of keys whose locks were long since been lost. The old man reached for a pen and card tag and in neat handwriting labeled the object as 'Kabbot' and placed it in front of the object.

The shopkeeper's focus was once again shifted towards the ledger he was glancing earlier. But somewhere deep down, he could not shake the feeling of uneasiness he got from the presence of the 'Kabbot'. There was a slight hum almost so low that he thought he might have imagined it. He tried to forget about the 'Kabbot' and returned to what he had been doing before the fisherman had entered his shop.

The afternoon sun was settling down, the heat being swapped with the cool air. A glint of light passed through the window and fell over the Kabbot making it appear extremely beautiful.

The wooden door of Time Machine creaked open, causing the rusted bell above to jangle out a strained, metallic chime. The antique store smelled of old parchment, aged wood, and the faintest trace of incense; a scent that lingered in the folds of time itself.

Vela stepped inside, her sharp blue eyes darting around the space with the practiced ease of someone accustomed to searching for hidden treasures. Her dark brown hair tied in a loose braid. She moved with a quiet confidence, her tall frame wrapped in a weathered brown coat. A bag hung loosely from her shoulder, filled with notebooks, maps, and a few odd trinkets she had picked up during her travels.

She loved places like these. Not the pristine, curated museums of the world, but the forgotten corners where the past sat gathering dust, waiting for someone to listen to its whispers.

The shelves bowed under the weight of history. Tarnished brass compasses, pocket watches frozen in time, intricately carved figurines from cultures long faded into legend. Stacks of yellowed parchment, rolled maps with corners curled from age, rusted astrolabes, and mysterious mechanical devices whose purposes had been long lost. The shop was a labyrinth of curiosity, an organized chaos where every object had once meant something to someone.

Vela's fingers trailed over an old globe, its colors faded, the names of countries outdated. She turned it slightly, her eyes lingering on the vastness of the Pacific. A subconscious pull, perhaps fate or mere chance, made her glance to the right, where a narrow shelf held a collection of peculiar artifacts.

And then she saw it.

It was small, barely the size of her palm, resting between a brass sextant and an ancient leather-bound book with an unreadable script on its spine. The object had a silvery-grey surface, but as the light from a nearby oil lamp flickered across it, a mesmerizing spectrum of colors danced beneath its sheen. The grooves on its surface twisted into delicate, organic spirals, almost like the intricate layers of a cut cabbage, yet smoother, more deliberate, as if crafted rather than formed naturally.

Vela reached out, lifting it carefully, rolling it between her fingers. It was heavier than she had expected, its weight solid and cool against her skin. As she turned it over, the iridescence shifted like a living thing, as though the metal itself breathed with color.

Her heart quickened slightly.

This was not ordinary.

She turned towards the counter, where the old shopkeeper watched her with a knowing glint in his eye. He had been observing her since she entered, as he did with every customer; silent, waiting, measuring the worth of their curiosity.

"How much for this?" she asked, holding up the object.

The old Chinese man leaned forward, his elbows resting on the counter. His face, a landscape of wrinkles and wisdom, twisted into an amused smile. His lone broken tooth was more visible now as he chuckled, a deep, almost gravelly sound, like an echo from another time.

"For you," he said slowly, "special price."

Vela smirked. "You mean an overcharged price."

The old man chuckled again, his heavy voice laced with mirth.

"You bargain, then? Tell me... how much is curiosity worth to you?"

She raised an eyebrow. This was a game she knew well.

She exhaled, crossing her arms. "I'd say about ten."

The shopkeeper clicked his tongue, shaking his head. "Ten? Hah! You insult the ancestors. This... this is no ordinary object. It has a history, you see. A mystery. History is priceless."

"Then why sell it at all?" she countered, tilting her head. "Unless... you don't know what it is either."

The old man's expression didn't change, but there was something in his eyes, just for a flicker of a moment—that told her she had struck a nerve.

"You are clever," he admitted. "Fifteen."

"Twelve."

"Fourteen."

She sighed theatrically, shaking her head. "Alright. Fourteen."

The old man nodded in satisfaction as she reached into her satchel and pulled out the worn leather pouch where she kept her coins. She counted out fourteen and placed them in his outstretched hand. His fingers, gnarled with age, closed around them before he gestured for her to wait.

From beneath the counter, he pulled out a small cloth wrap. With deliberate care, he placed the silvery object inside and folded the fabric around it. Then, he slid it across the counter toward her.

Vela picked it up, feeling the weight in her hand. "Does it have a name?" she asked.

The shopkeeper gave a slow nod. "Kabbot."

Her brow furrowed. "Kabbot?"

He tapped the wooden counter absentmindedly. "A name I gave it. You see, every object must have a name, or it is forgotten. And forgotten things... well, they are lost forever."

Vela studied him for a moment before she tucked the wrapped object into her satchel. "Well, let's hope I don't forget it."

She turned to leave, but as she reached the door, the old man's voice, deep and ancient, drifted through the shop.

"Curiosity, young traveler, is a dangerous thing."

She glanced back over her shoulder. His expression was unreadable.

With a small nod, she stepped out into the bustling market, the weight of the Kabbot resting against her hip. Feeling the Kabbot in her bag she asked it as if it could hear her and reply to her question, "What are you?"

She had no idea that in her hands lay something far greater than just a peculiar trinket.

Something that would change everything.

★★

Far from the bustling crowds and the hustling market, was the ship getting ready to sail. The International Consortium of Marine Research (ICMR) team was gathering around the port. The mission was steeped in secrecy, whispered about only in hushed tones among certain scientific circles. It was not merely about studying marine ecosystems or mapping unknown territories—it was about investigating phenomena that defied conventional understanding. Reports of strange occurrences, unexplained environmental anomalies, and sightings of peculiar underwater structures had intrigued the Consortium. Their goal was to seek answers where others had failed to look, and this team was the spearhead of that endeavor.

The group had convened in the bustling heart of a coastal market for their final preparations. Dr. Richard Stones, the expedition leader, stood slightly apart from the commotion, his tall frame and silver-streaked hair making him an imposing figure. Stones had an air of authority about him, the kind that came from years of leadership in extreme environments. His sharp eyes, always alert, darted across his team as they busied themselves with their tasks. His quiet yet commanding presence and his ability to remain composed under pressure had made him an invaluable leader.

Tim, the gadget expert, was a man of quiet focus. His glasses have a slight crack in one lens from an old lab accident, and his dark, unruly hair makes it clear that he cares little for appearances. A genius in his own right, is both a scientist and an engineer, specializing in electromagnetic fields and unexplained energy anomalies.

Beside him, Rox, the team's botanist. A quiet observer of nature with an unmatched fascination for flora. Her short brown hair and black pants are perpetually dusted with soil, and her dark green eyes are constantly scanning the environment for new discoveries. Though introverted, Rox is fiercely protective of nature, detesting unnecessary destruction for the sake of science.

Nearby, Emo, a linguist with an insatiable appetite for ancient texts. Her specialty was decoding languages long forgotten, and her expertise would be crucial if the team encountered remnants of unknown civilizations. Lean and sun-kissed from years of fieldwork, she has an almost obsessive focus when studying artifacts, often losing herself in her research.

Jones, stocky with sun-worn skin and perpetually salt crusted hair. He always carries himself with the confidence of someone who has spent years battling the unpredictability of the sea. Having worked on classified oceanic projects involving undiscovered marine species and deep-sea anomalies, he is familiar with the feeling of staring into the abyss and seeing something stare back. Jones is meticulous in his observations but quick to dismiss anything unscientific.

A woman of quiet intensity, Carrey, has made a career out of analyzing human responses in extreme environments. Her piercing grey eyes and carefully neutral expressions hide the constant assessments running through her mind. Having worked with astronauts, arctic explorers, and deep-sea divers, she understands better than anyone how isolation and fear warp the human psyche. Her primary role is to monitor the team's emotional and mental well-being, ensuring that paranoia doesn't take hold.

Ted, is the quiet backbone of the operation, processing data and ensuring every discovery is recorded accurately. With light brown hair and glasses perpetually sliding down his nose, he rarely speaks unless necessary. He prefers numbers to people, believing that data never lies.

Efficient, pragmatic, and intolerant of disorganization, Lisa, the backbone that keeps the expedition from spiraling into chaos. Her sleek black hair is always tied in a neat bun, and her dark brown eyes are constantly scanning her data terminal.

She does not allow distractions or inefficiency to slow the team down. As the project manager, she ensures that findings are documented, reports are transmitted, and funding remains intact. She believes in results, not speculation, which puts her at odds with those who seek mystery rather than clarity.

Anarina, the zoologist, adjusted her binoculars, observing the activity around her with the practiced eye of someone used to studying wildlife. Her gaze lingered on the unusual birds darting above the market, their colors shimmering in the sunlight. She had a way of finding patterns and connections in the smallest details, and her insights had often led to breakthroughs on past expeditions.

Stones clapped his hands together sharply, cutting through the din. "Let's move!" he commanded, his voice clear and resolute. The team sprang into action, gathering their supplies and making their way towards the harbor. There, moored against the docks, awaited their vessel: The Mercy of Seas.

"The Mercy of Seas" stood like a titan against the horizon, her hull reinforced to withstand the might of the ocean. The ship had been designed for both research and endurance, outfitted with cutting-edge technology. Submersibles, sonar scanners, pressurized labs—it had everything needed to delve into the depths of the unknown.

As the last of the supplies were loaded, Mr. Jones, the chief marine biologist, gathered the crew for a final briefing.

"From this moment on, we are on an expedition unlike any before," he declared, his voice cutting through the salty wind. "This is not just another research mission. The ocean holds secrets we've barely scratched the surface of. Our goal is to uncover those secrets while ensuring the safety of this crew."

A final check was performed: equipment secured, maps studied, last-minute calibrations done. With a resounding call from the captain, the engines rumbled to life.

The ship drifted away from the docks, carried by the tide into the open ocean.

Each of them carried their own hopes, fears, and questions about the mission ahead.

Tim leaned against the railing, gazing out at the open sea. "You think we'll find it?" he asked, breaking the silence.

"Find what?" Rox replied, turning her attention from a notebook where she'd been sketching the coastal plants.

"Whatever it is we're out here looking for," Tim said, gesturing vaguely toward the horizon. "The reports, the anomalies, it's all so... vague."

"We're not looking for one thing," Stones interjected, his voice calm but firm. "We're looking for answers. Whatever form they take."

The team nodded, their leader's words grounding them.

The coastline faded. The horizon stretched endlessly.

The expedition had begun.

And beyond that horizon, something unseen waited, something ancient, something watching.

The Mercy of Seas cut through the waters, its reinforced hull slicing through the undulating waves like a blade. The air was thick with the scent of salt and freedom, and for the first few days, the voyage was nothing short of magnificent. The water stretched endlessly in every direction, its surface a vast mirror reflecting the changing moods of the sky.

The ICMR team, each absorbed in their respective tasks, quickly fell into the rhythm of the expedition. Stones spent most of his time in the ship's research bay, pondering over old maritime maps and legends, searching for any record of uncharted islands or strange occurrences. Rox meticulously cataloged samples of seaweed and airborne spores, analyzing their unique compositions. Juno was thrilled to inspect any fossilized remains found along the seabed during deep-sea trawling. Tim, the scientist, studied changes in water temperature, salinity, and unusual sonar readings, while Anarina logged patterns in marine life behavior.

The ship's crew, experienced sailors who had braved the ocean's fury time and again, kept a close eye on the weather. Lisa, the project manager, ensured that every detail of the mission was executed with precision. Hills, the medical expert, monitored the health of the team, mindful of the toll that long voyages could take. Carrey, the psychologist, observed the growing excitement—and underlying tension—that came with such a journey.

For a while, the sea was their ally, smooth and cooperative. But on the third day, the sky began to shift.

The first sign of trouble came in the form of an unnatural stillness. The once playful waves became heavy, sluggish, as though the ocean itself was holding its breath. The wind, once a gentle whisper, vanished completely. The crew exchanged uneasy glances, their instincts honed from years at sea warning them of what was to come.

Then, without warning, the sky darkened. Thick, ominous clouds rolled in from the west, swallowing the sun. The temperature dropped sharply, and an eerie silence fell over the ship.

It came suddenly, a roar of wind, so fierce it felt like a living beast had been unleashed from the heavens. The ocean, once calm, erupted in violent chaos. Waves surged like towering walls of liquid fury, crashing against the ship with the force of an earthquake.

Keeping the ship together during a storm so bad was almost impossible. Everyone held onto each other and in their own field of expertise tried to handle the situation to the best of their abilities.

Lightning split the sky in jagged, blinding streaks, followed by thunder so loud it rattled their bones. The rain struck like thousands of tiny daggers, cold and unrelenting.

In the midst of the storm, Jones clung to the ship's railing, his mind racing. "This storm isn't natural!" he shouted over the howling wind.

Anarina, drenched to the bone, nodded. "The patterns—this isn't like any recorded storm. It's erratic, but... almost deliberate."

Below deck, Lisa was shouting orders, securing equipment and stabilizing loose objects. Tim struggled to keep their instruments online, his hands steady despite the violent lurching of the ship.

Mr. Stones, usually a man of logic, had an unsettling thought. "It's like something doesn't want us here," he murmured, gripping the armrest of his chair as the ship trembled under another brutal wave.

The storm did not relent.

For four days, the ocean punished them. Four days of relentless wind and crushing waves. Sleep was impossible, food scarce, morale stretched to its limits. Injuries were inevitable—Hills worked tirelessly, treating cuts, bruises, and exhaustion. Even Carrey, the psychologist, struggled to keep everyone's spirits afloat.

By the fifth day, something changed.

The wind began to die down. The waves no longer crashed but rolled lazily, as if drained of their fury. The clouds, once thick and impenetrable, began to thin, allowing slivers of golden sunlight to pierce through. The ocean returned to its former calm, as if the storm had never happened at all.

It was as if... it had led them somewhere. It felt as if the sea was testing them to see if they were fit to enter the island and do their research.

A collective gasp rippled through the crew as they gathered on the deck, eyes locked onto the horizon.

There, rising from the mist, was an island.

But not just any island.

It was unlike anything they had seen before. Towering cliffs of obsidian-black stone jutted out from the water, partially veiled by thick, silver mist. The dense jungle beyond pulsed with glowing flora, bioluminescent plants casting an ethereal blue-green shimmer. Strange bird-like creatures with iridescent feathers flitted between trees, their songs unlike any known species. A faint hum, low and rhythmic, seemed to resonate through the air itself, as though the very ground thrummed with an ancient, forgotten energy.

Vines, thick and sinewy, coiled around massive trees, their leaves shimmering like molten metal. The water surrounding the island was unnaturally clear, revealing coral formations that seemed to glow beneath the surface, pulsating as though alive.

"Impossible..." Juno whispered, his voice barely audible. "This place... it shouldn't exist."

Mr. Stones stood frozen, eyes wide. "There's no record of this island on any chart. No satellite data. Nothing. It's like it was never here before."

Lisa turned to the others and doubtfully asked. "Are we still on course? Maybe we drifted off during the storm?"

Stones shook his head, bewildered. "No. This island... it wasn't here before. I swear it. We are on the right page. This is the very island that has no history as to how it came to life, what it is called or in fact any information related to it is not available."

The team exchanged glances. Fear, awe, and curiosity warred within them.

Jones, always the pragmatist, broke the silence. "We need to go ashore. We came here for discovery, and we just found something worth a thousand lifetimes of study."

The team began preparations, lowering their research gear, assembling a plan. Some hesitated, but their hunger for knowledge overcame their trepidation.

The ship was anchored and all the members got on in smaller boats. With each paddle stroke, the team edged closer to the shoreline. The air was charged, as if the island itself was watching them.

The ICMR team, an elite force of the world's greatest minds, had set out to uncover the secrets of the ocean.

But some secrets should remain buried.

And this island...

It was probably never meant to be found.

They reached the shore and slowly started to go along with all the tools and equipment that they had carried with themselves. Exhaustion was clearly visible on their faces but it was well hidden under the excitement of being on an absolutely unknown island.

They brought their equipment to the base and started setting up their camps. Tents were erected in a semi-circle, their reflective surfaces catching the light from the glowing sands. Equipment was unpacked and sorted, each piece carefully checked after the storm. Stones directed the activity with his usual efficiency, his calm presence steadying the team.

The sun began to set and over the horizon it looked absolutely pretty with beautiful shades of orange and yellow. The faint glow of the jungle intensified, the foliage pulsing with a bioluminescence that cast shifting patterns of light across the beach. Strange sounds filled the air—chirps, hums, and guttural calls that seemed to come from every direction at once. The team, huddled around a small cooking station, exchanged uneasy glances.

"This place..." Rox began, her voice trailing off. She shook her head, unable to find the words.

"It's alive," Emo finished for her, her tone equal parts awe and trepidation.

"It's watching us," Anarina added, her eyes scanning the tree line.

Stones, sensing the growing tension, spoke up. "Get some rest," he said firmly. "Tomorrow, we will explore. Keep your wits about you. We don't know what we're dealing with, but we'll face it together."

The team retreated to their tents, though few found sleep easy to come by. Outside, the sounds of the island seemed to grow louder, closer, as if testing the boundaries of their camp. The faint hum that Vela had felt from the Kabbot, now safely stored in one of the crates, seemed to resonate with the pulses of light from the jungle, creating an eerie harmony that no one dared to acknowledge.

Something about the island did not feel right. Rox felt as if they were not alone. She felt the presence of someone even though there was no one. She could hear the sounds of rustling voices and faint hums coming from outside her tent. As she switched on the torch, there was nothing. All the other members had already gone back to their tents and were probably asleep as well after such an adventurous journey.

The night crept in but the uneasiness hadn't slept.

Chapter 2

Pillars of Oynm

The morning sun cast long shadows over the remote island, its golden rays filtering through the dense canopy of towering trees. The rhythmic crashing of waves against the shoreline provided a steady backdrop to the expedition's preparations. The base camp, set up the previous evening near a freshwater stream, was now bustling with activity. Tents flapped in the morning breeze, metallic crates of equipment gleamed in the sunlight, and a cooking fire crackled, sending up spirals of smoke.

The sun rays created an amber glow across the wilderness. The flora that glowed the previous night began to dim as though retreating into the shadows. Everyone had slept through the night but none looked fresh.

All the members had gathered at the centre of the campsite where the aromatic smell of coffee mingled with the salty sea breeze. A few stretched out sore muscles whereas a few just sat with their morning coffee with thoughts of the previous night lingering in their minds.

Looking at everyone's tensed face, Tim asked, "Did anyone hear any sounds last night or was I the only one who had such imaginations?"

No one responded though they all very well knew that Tim wasn't the only one who had heard.

Vela took her time but hesitantly responded, "This isn't imagination. The island has something that it is hiding and something is very mysterious about the island."

The conversation was interrupted by the commanding voice of Stones, their expedition leader. He stood with his arms crossed, his leather-bound journal tucked under one arm, surveying the team with a seasoned explorer's gaze. Behind him, a long wooden table had been set up, lined with neatly arranged trekking bags, each customized with tools specific to the expedition members' fields of expertise. The air buzzed with anticipation as the team prepared for the day's mission.

Stones clapped his hands together, calling for attention. "Alright, listen up. This is uncharted territory. We need to be efficient, observant, and above all, cautious. You'll each receive an exploration kit, tailored to your area of expertise. These are your lifelines out here, use them wisely."

With that, he gestured toward the table and began handing out the kits one by one, taking a moment to lock eyes with each team member, silently reminding them of their individual responsibilities.

Each bag contained standard expedition essentials: lightweight, moisture-wicking t-shirts embroidered with the team insignia, reinforced trekking bags with waterproof compartments, self-filtering water bottles, portable radios, emergency kits stocked with basic first-aid supplies, and multi-tools equipped with a foldable knife, fire starter, and rope. These were survival necessities, but each kit also contained specialized equipment suited to the expertise of its recipient.

Lisa, adjusting her oversized field binoculars. Her geochemical scanner hummed softly in her pack, strapped alongside a spectrometer, environmental gauge, and a small medical kit. Along with those a notebook she kept with her set of stationary to note down as a project head. Her backpack was blue in colour with the ICMR tag and label.

Rox received a dark green bag with a leaf emblem. Inside, she found airtight specimen containers, a compact but powerful portable microscope, and chemical analysis vials. A soil pH and moisture test kit had been included to help her understand the composition of the terrain, along with sterile gloves and cutting tools for safely handling unknown flora. A UV light scanner was tucked neatly inside, useful for detecting bioluminescent plants hidden in the undergrowth. As she ran her fingers over the smooth case of the microscope, she felt a thrill of anticipation, whatever secrets the jungle held, she was ready to uncover them.

Tim accepted his kit with a skeptical smirk. His sturdy black bag was packed with an array of high-tech instruments: an energy scanner to detect anomalies, precision measurement devices including a digital altimeter and laser rangefinder, a portable weather monitor, and a radiation detector. A rugged field laptop, waterproof and shockproof, was secured inside, preloaded with data-logging software. As he adjusted his glasses and slung the bag over his shoulder, he muttered, "If anything on this island is messing with our instruments, I'll find it."

Emo carefully opened her bag to reveal a collection of ancient translation lexicons, a thick notebook and graphite pencils for sketching symbols, and a reading lens with a built-in LED light for examining fine details. She also had carbon rubbing sheets for tracing inscriptions without damaging them and a voice recorder to capture any strange sounds or whispers. As she adjusted the strap of her bag, she murmured, "I'll be listening to the stories that this island is going to tell."

Juno took his dust-colored bag without a word, his fingers instinctively running over the well-worn fabric. Inside, he found rock chisels and hammers, a soil sample kit, and a UV fluorescence lamp to detect minerals with unusual properties. A seismic scanner, capable of detecting ground disturbances and mapping underground formations, was tucked securely inside. A magnetic sensor had also been included, its purpose clear—if there was any unusual geological activity on this island, it wouldn't stay hidden for long.

Anarina's zoologist's kit, slung across her back in a compact but efficient weatherproof bag, contained everything she needed to study the island's strange fauna. A digital field notebook & sketching pad, thermal-imaging binoculars, ultrasonic sound recorder, handheld bioscanner, tranq-dart pen & specimen vials and a portable motion detector which would be useful for detecting predators or unseen creatures watching them.

Inside his heavy-duty military-style backpack with the label and tag of ICMR, Hills carried: a portable solar charger, Multi-tool & repair kit, emergency medical pouch, topographical maps & navigation tools, basic excavation tools, energy bars & hydration packs.

Being a researcher and a psychologist, Carrey carried a digital research tablet, compact sample vials and chemical test strips, graphite rubbing sheets and precision stylus, backup audio recorder and a luminol spray and UV light scanner.

Lastly Jones picked up his bag and opened it to find a portable water analysis kit, handheld sonar scanner, retractable sampling net and containment vials, lightweight rebreather mask if at all he would have to go within the waters and a magnetic depth gauge as a backup tool to measure changes manually.

The kits distributed, Stones took a moment to meet each person's gaze, ensuring they understood their responsibilities. His expression was serious, but there was an undercurrent of something else; determination, perhaps even reverence. This was not just an expedition. It was a discovery waiting to unfold.

"We're stepping into the unknown," Stones said. "This island wasn't meant to be found, and we're about to find out why." His voice carried a quiet intensity as he added, "No one goes off alone. No unnecessary risks. Stay in radio contact. And whatever happens—trust your instincts."

No words were exchanged as the weight of what Stones had just said settled in. The island ahead was silent and the whispers they had heard clung onto their memory. One by one, the team secured their bags, adjusted their gear, and prepared to move out. The jungle ahead felt different now, as though it had been watching all along. Stones took one last look at his team, then gave a single, resolute nod.

"Let's begin."

As they stepped beyond the boundaries of the camp and into the wilderness, the trees whispered in the wind, and somewhere in the distance, something stirred.

The island grew thicker as the team ventured beyond the perimeter of the base camp and entered a place that looked more like a jungle. The soft crackle of leaves underfoot mixed with the distant sounds of creatures that had not yet been classified by science. Sunlight pierced through the gaps in the foliage, casting shifting patterns on the damp ground as if the jungle itself was alive, watching, waiting.

Everyone was convinced that the island was slowly revealing itself to them intentionally as to wanting them to see something.

Rox wandered through the jungle with her journal in one hand and explored the flora that was extraordinary and something never seen before. The glow in the plants she had seen the previous night was nothing similar to what she was seeing at that moment. Her breath hitched as she stepped closer, brushing aside a tangle of vines to reveal a stunning sight; a cluster of ferns pulsating with iridescent blue veins, as if their very cells were charged with an inner light.

She carefully cut through a small section of the glowing plant and placed it inside the specimen container. But that glow started to fade and flicker as soon as it was cut and placed within the container. It flickered like a heartbeat slowing down. Rox froze, watching as the plants responded to her actions.

Her mind raced. Are these plants communicating and Sharing energy?

She reached into her bag for her portable microscope, setting the glowing leaf on the slide. Adjusting the lens, she gasped.

Inside the cells of the plant, bioluminescent filaments pulsed in a synchronized pattern, aligning like some neural network.

While Rox was in the jungle, Anarina crouched near a natural clearing. Adjusting her binoculars as she tracked movement in the trees ahead. At first, she thought she was watching primate-like creatures, given their agility and the way they clung to the branches. But as one leapt into full view, her breath caught in her throat.

The creature had four limbs, but they weren't primate-like at all. Its body was covered in fine, translucent fur that shimmered when it moved, and its eyes, large, black, and unblinking, glowed faintly even in daylight.

Then, the others emerged, a pack of them, moving in perfect synchronization, never breaking eye contact with Anarina.

★★

Juno had been digging at the base of a rocky outcrop, chiseling away layers of sediment in search of unusual mineral compositions. His seismic scanner had detected anomalous readings in the area, signs of something hollow beneath the surface.

As he drove his pickaxe into the rock, a deep reverberation shuddered through the ground.

He froze.

Then he did it again.

Thud. Thud.

The ground responded.

Juno's breath hitched as he pressed his palm to the stone. Beneath his hand, the rock was warm.

Then, it moved.

Not shifted, not crumbled. The rock expanded and contracted, like it was breathing.

His instincts screamed for him to pull away, but his scientist's mind refused. He grabbed his scanner, measuring the vibrations. His device flickered, its readings erratic, showing energy patterns that shouldn't exist in rock formations.

★★

Tim, Emo, and Lisa walked cautiously, with Tim leading the way, his scanner in hand. The trek had been uneventful until now, just standard jungle terrain, damp and humid, the air thick with the scent of moss and earth. But then, as they descended into a clearing, Tim's device began blinking erratically.

"Hold up," he muttered, frowning at the screen. He tapped the buttons, adjusting the settings. The energy readings were off the charts, and yet there was no visible source. "Something's wrong here."

Emo slowed her steps, peering ahead. The clearing was unnatural: a perfectly circular space, devoid of dense vegetation, its ground layered with smooth, dark stones. And at its center stood seven towering monoliths, arranged in a V-shape, each standing precisely 50 meters apart.

Lisa inhaled sharply. "This is... incredible."

The pillars loomed, ancient and weathered, their surfaces carved with intricate geometric patterns and symbols. Their surfaces smooth, but cracked with age. Vines had begun to creep up their sides, yet something about them defied nature itself, as if the jungle knew better than to reclaim them entirely.

Tim stepped forward cautiously. His scanner flickered and then shut off completely. At the same moment, his compass needle began to spin wildly, pointing in impossible directions.

"What the hell—?" He took a step back. The moment he did, his devices returned to normal. He stepped forward again, and once more, his equipment failed completely. He took a step back again to see if they get back to normal but this time no result.

"Okay, that's not normal."

Emo barely heard him. Her focus had shifted entirely to the symbols on the nearest pillar. The carvings weren't just decorative, they were writing. An ancient script, almost mathematical in design, its shapes precise yet impossibly complex. She instinctively reached for her sketchpad, pulling it free as she traced a careful finger over the stone. She tried to decode and figured something like Pillars of Oynm written and guessed it was the name of the seven pillars.

A moment of silence and all three of them heard something. It was more like an eerie whisper. Lisa's face could tell that it was not some normal sound. Their hearts pounding fast and the humming becoming clearer than ever in the silence.

"Did you hear that?" asked Lisa. She strained to listen. The words were faint, like a voice speaking just beyond the veil of comprehension.

"Know where to see..."

Her breath caught. "Did you hear that?"

Lisa shivered. "It sounded like..."

She hesitated, glancing at Tim.

Tim frowned. "I didn't hear 'Know where to see.' I heard... 'Nowhere to see.'"

They exchanged looks, their previous confidence starting to unravel.

The whispers didn't stop.

They grew louder.

The air itself felt heavy, charged with an invisible force. The pillars stood unchanging, yet the sensation that something was watching them was undeniable.

Tim exhaled sharply, shaking his head. "I'm calling Stones."

He grabbed his radio, his voice slightly strained as he pressed the button. "Base camp, this is Tim. We have a situation."

A crackle of static. Then, Stones' calm but firm voice came through. "Report."

Tim didn't hesitate. "We found something. Seven pillars. They're ancient. They're... messing with our instruments, and Emo says they're whispering."

There was a pause.

Then Stones' voice returned, sharp and decisive. "Return to base camp immediately."

★★

As the sun started to set, the team made their way back to the camp with their set of discoveries. The weight of what they had seen and heard had settled deep within them. They were welcomed with a tensed Stones waiting for them at the entrance of the campsite.

Everyone gathered around the large table that had been set up at the center of the camp with maps, sketches, data sheets and space kept available for all the samples that were collected. The fire in the centre of the table illuminated their faces giving light to the paleness that had already begun to appear.

Rox set down her specimen case, carefully retrieving a sealed vial containing the glowing fern sample she had taken earlier. She placed it under the portable microscope, adjusting the focus.

"Look at this," she said, turning the lens toward the others.

The team gathered around as the microscopic view projected onto the tablet screen. The plant's cells pulsed in synchronized waves, moving as if responding to an unseen rhythm.

"This isn't just photosynthesis or bioluminescence," Rox explained, her voice thick with excitement. "These plants are communicating—transmitting energy between them, like neurons in a brain."

A hush fell over the group.

Tim, frowning, leaned in. "You're saying this jungle is... connected? A single, living system?"

Rox nodded. "I don't know, it's all just an assumption. Nothing can be concluded."

Listening to what Rox just said about her discovery, Juno added, "I don't know about you guys, but I put my hand on a rock today, and it almost felt like it breathed."

Carrey scoffed. "Breathed?"

"I'm serious," Juno insisted. He laid out his seismic scanner's readings. "This outcrop wasn't just radiating heat—it was expanding and contracting, like a living thing. And the frequencies it emitted? Unlike anything we've ever documented."

Emo furrowed her brows. "Could it be volcanic activity?"

Juno shook his head. "If it were that simple, I wouldn't be this shaken. It wasn't random vibrations. It was rhythmic. Deliberate."

The group exchanged uneasy glances.

Anarina cleared her throat, her fingers still tense around her sketchbook. "I saw something watching us today," she said carefully. "Not an animal—not in the way we define them."

She turned her notebook toward the group to show the detailed sketch of what she had observed.

"They don't just see," she continued, her voice lower now. "They... see into us. I could feel them watching. And I heard something—"

Stones' eyes snapped up. "You heard something?"

She hesitated. "It wasn't sound. It was like... a whisper. In my mind. A voice that said, 'You see us now.'"

The team stiffened as they looked at the images of the samples and extraordinaries clicked by Ed.

Out of all the ICMR members present in that moment at that place, Tim, Emo and Lisa looked completely drained after listening to the discoveries of the others.

Tim gestured toward the sketch of the monolithic pillars, carefully drawn by Emo, and spread out a set of disorganized readings from his scanner.

"We found something big," he said, his usual sarcasm absent. "Seven massive stone pillars, arranged in a V-shape, each spaced exactly 50 meters apart. They're ancient—probably older than anything on this island."

He tapped his scanner, shaking his head. "But here's the problem—when I went near those my equipment stopped working and then when I went far from it, it worked. I tried that again and then it completely shut down. My compass spun out of control, my energy scanner went haywire."

Stones' brows furrowed. "Magnetic interference?"

"Maybe," Tim admitted. "But that's not all." He turned to Emo. "Tell them what you heard."

Emo adjusted her reading glasses, swallowing. "The pillars... They hum. It's subtle at first, but if you listen closely, they start to whisper."

Stones' face darkened. "What did they say?"

Emo exhaled, flipping through her notebook until she found the page. She had written the phrase in bold, hurried strokes:

"Nowhere to see."

The team read it in silence.

Then Lisa spoke softly, "That's not what I heard."

Everyone turned toward her.

Lisa hesitated before saying, "I heard it differently. I thought they were saying: 'Know where to see.'"

A chill passed over the group.

Tim crossed his arms. "Are we sure it wasn't just static? Our brains are filling in the blanks?"

"No," Emo said, her voice tight. "This wasn't static. It was deliberate. The pillars were speaking to us."

"Maybe it's just in our minds," stated Ed.

Silence fell over the base camp. No one knew what to understand and comprehend out of all the discoveries. Was the island trying to tell them something? Was what they heard actually true or was it just something they imagined.

Breaking the silence, Stones said ,"We need to break into teams and discover the island and find out the truth it is trying to hide."

Team Explore would have the task to investigate the natural formations on the left side of the pillars.

Members: Juno (geologist and paleontologist), Anarina (zoologist and linguist), Carrey (researcher and psychologist), Hills (medical expert and field assistant), Vela (explorer and an intern).

Team Discover would study the right side Whispering Pillars and any possible connections to the island's history.

Members: Stones (leader), Emo (linguist and archeologist), Lisa (project manager), Tim (scientist and gadget expert), Ed (photographer and intern).

Team Research would stay at base camp to analyze collected samples and organize data.

Members: Rox (botanist), Jones (marine biologist), Ted (data analyst).

The team nodded, knowing this was the only logical next step.

Stones folded his arms. "We need answers, and fast. We move first thing in the morning. No one ventures out alone. No unnecessary risks. And if anything—anything—seems wrong, we regroup immediately."

The team broke apart, preparing for the next phase of the mission. Some went to analyze their findings, while others tended to their equipment. But no one truly relaxed.

As night descended, the jungle's familiar hum returned, but this time... something was different.

From deep within the forest, near the pillars, a single, resonant tone rang out, vibrating through the earth.

But fortunately or not no one at the base camp could hear it.

The jungle had been watching.

And now, it was calling them back.

Chapter 3

Ruins of Suryl

The sun cast its sunlight beautifully over the base camp. The usual hum of the insects was still there and nothing about it had changed except the mood on the island. The once energetic members were now tensed with all the happenings they had witnessed in just one day.

Team Discover got ready and gathered at the centre of the base camp. Their backpacks strapped on, radios checked and all the necessary supplies secured. They were not sure what they were going to encounter next but had to be well prepared.

Their walk towards the 7 pillars began. The view and the landscape was extremely serene. Those who visited the pillars the previous day were so lost in their discovery that they had not even noticed the view. The mountains, flora and the fauna they witnessed was something beyond their imagination. The lush greenery on either side bloomed with such beauty that one could spend half a day just sitting there or just wander about.

Amidst the peace, Stones reminded the others in the team "Alright, listen up, we have to be careful as we go forward, we don't know what's in store for us or what we are going to meet. So we need to make sure that we are always together and don't wander-"

Before he could complete his sentence, Lisa shouted "Look at that butterfly. It looks like a completely different species as if it does not even belong to the butterfly clan. The way it is glowing even in broad daylight is something extraordinary."

Emo reacted as quickly as Lisa shouted. With her palm on her chest she said "What is wrong with you? You could have said that softly and not give a minor attack."

Not listening to Emo, Lisa continued, "Look at its wings carefully, it's not something that a normal butterfly would look like. It has long and brighter wings that glow in the sunlight."

Tim added with a playful smirk on his face, "When we are all trying to uncover a mystery, Lisa the project head is head over heels for a butterfly."

"It's better than pulling a long face and thinking about all the weird happenings on this island. It's called a change of mind, being calm and forgetting about all that's bothering." Lisa shot back.

To not let this argument escalate, Stones stepped in and said, "Guys all jokes aside now, focus on the trek. It is not an easy route, better watch out and make sure not to hurt yourself. At the same time keep your eyes open for any new discovery you make."

Silence fell upon. Everyone peacefully walked along the trail making notes of what they saw.

The trail was a narrow path along the lush green forest. Trees stretched high forming a canopy overhead. The air was cool and fresh, filled with the scent of damp earth and the flora. The sound of birds chirping and the rustling of the leaves filled the silent path with noise. Tiny white and yellow butterflies flitted between colorful wildflowers, and a small brook bubbled beside the path, its clear water reflecting the sky.

Soon that trail was replaced with a rocky uneven path, giving way to tall cliffs and jagged hills. It was something that was not even discovered the previous day. The change gave way to a rough climb, with loose stones and tree roots that could trip you if you were not attentive.

Lisa, stepping carefully over a gnarled root, huffed, "Okay, is this still a hike, or did we sign up for an obstacle course?"

Tim, effortlessly hopping over a fallen log, grinned. "It's all about perspective."

Lisa narrowed her eyes. "My perspective says I should have stayed home."

To their left, the land sloped down into a deep valley, where a hidden waterfall crashed into a shimmering lake below. The sound of rushing water echoed through the canyon, mixing with the distant calls of hawks circling overhead.

To their right, the path grew narrow, hugging the edge of a steep cliffside. One wrong step here, and it was a long tumble down to sharp rocks below.

Emo, glancing down, muttered, "You know, I really don't love how close we are to falling to our deaths."

Ed, walking ahead, shrugged. "Well, at least it's a scenic way to go."

Lisa groaned. "Can we not talk about dying while we're literally inches from disaster?"

After an hour or so they came across a ruin. On the huge structure was something scribbled in an alien language. Emo took her time to come to a conclusion and declare what it was called, "Ruins of Suryl" she said finally after spending almost 15 minutes on it.

Entering in the ruins left them all in shock. They could not believe what they were seeing. Their eyes wide open, mouths open in shock and their stance fixed in one position before Lisa broke the silence. "Let's go and check what we can get out of this ruin. A lot seems to be hidden within these crystalized formations."

The formations seemed to have buried a lot of secrets that were untold and uncovered but would have had much crucial information.

From afar those towering formations looked like stones. The team stepped closer, realization settling over them like a thick fog.

Inside the transparent crystal formations, warriors stood locked in combat, their expressions frozen in time. Some were mid-swing, their weapons suspended in the air. Others had already fallen, their faces twisted in agony. The battlefield scenarios had been preserved within these glacial tombs, a moment of war captured for eternity.

"This is..." Ed hesitated, pressing a hand against the cold surface of a nearby crystal, "Surreal."

Emo traced the insignia carved into the crystalline surface, "It's the same marking as the one on the pillars."

"Are you sure?" asked Stones.

"Of course," assured Emo.

Tim pointed at one particularly brutal scene, his voice laced with disbelief. "Woah, that looks like a brutal one of a kind scene." Everyone turned to see what was something so extraordinary.

The scene before them depicted a hulking warrior; Sentori, the infamous rebel commander, clutching 80% of the Kabbot, the ancient artifact. His expression was one of grim determination, but his fate had already been sealed, standing before him, Elara, the King's most loyal warrior and Sentori's rival, equal in power but opposite intent. The scene before them was devastating in its detail. Sentori, his armor cracked and broken, had fallen to one knee. The spear in Elara's hand was buried deep in his side, and his face was frozen in agony. In his hand, the Kabbot fragment gleamed like a star against the darkness of the battlefield.

It looked so real as if it would come alive any moment. Ed involuntarily took a step back and his eyes widened at the recognition of the Kabbot in Sentori's hands.

Emo tilted her head. "Sentori had the Kabbot—most of it, but Elara took him down before he could use it."

Tim stepped closer. "If this is just a scene from the past... then where's the rest of the Kabbot now?"

"I've seen the rest of the Kabbot before," Ed said, his voice barely above a whisper.

Emo snapped his attention toward him. "What? Where?"

"In Vela's hands," Ed muttered, his mind racing. "Back at the other trail."

For a single heartbeat, the team stood frozen, just like the warriors before them.

Then, Ed took off at a sprint.

"Hey! Where are you—" Mr. Stones started, but it was already too late.

Tim groaned, watching Ed disappear down the left path. "Well. There goes our liability waiver."

Lisa groaned. "Oh great. Now we're chasing Ed."

Tim sighed, cracking his knuckles. "Guess that means we're running now."

Emo muttered, "I swear, we need to start keeping trackers on people in this group."

Mr. Stones, already moving, barked out a command, "Follow him. We don't leave anyone behind."

Chapter 4

Caves of Atumkhor

While team Discover looked around the ruins, team Explore consisting of Juno, Anarina, Carrey, Hills and Vela set out towards the other side of the pillars. Juno's backpack consisted of excavation tools and specimen jars, Anarina carried a notebook along with other necessities that she required to decode the language whenever required, Hills being the medical expert had the right medicines for any emergency. Being a psychologist, Carrey did not have much to carry except the bag given by Stones consisting of a safety kit. Vela, along with the emergency kit, had the Kabbot in her bag.

As they reached the pillars the plain grass was slowly switched with a breathtaking view of the island and its landscape, the beautiful flora and fauna covered in lush greenery. Mountains stretched far in the view covered in mist from the distance. The greenery glistening due to the sun and the flowers illuminated a different glow even in broad daylight.

Walking along the pillars gave them an eerie unexplainable energy.

Carrey froze. "Did anyone else hear that?"

The others turned. Anarina frowned. "Hear what?"

Carrey strained her ears. It was almost like whispering, but too subtle, as if the very air was murmuring secrets. "It's nothing... never mind." She shook off the eerie sensation and kept walking.

Juno and Anarina knelt down near the pillars to see the carvings and inscriptions. Pulling out her reading lens, Anarina jotted down a few things in her notebook, thinking it might be of help later in their expedition. Once she was done with noting down, they left for further discovery.

The trek beyond the pillars became even more exhausting. The terrain unpredictably shifted beneath their boots. The ground, loose with gravel and occasional sinkholes forcing them to tread carefully. Vines stretched along the jungle making it even more difficult for them to cross it safely.

Vela wiped sweat from her forehead as she stepped carefully over exposed tree roots. "I swear, this island was designed to break ankles," she muttered, adjusting the straps of her backpack.

Carrey smirked. "Maybe it's just testing our endurance before letting us in on its secrets."

As they trudged forward, the sounds of the jungle; chirping insects, rustling leaves, and distant animal cries, were gradually replaced by an eerie silence. A strange sensation settled over the group, an unspoken tension curling in their stomachs like a warning they couldn't quite articulate.

"Anyone else feeling like something is off about this place, leading to some distant place?" asked Hills.

Juno, leading the Team Explore warned, "Stay alert, we seem to be close to something uncovered and unknown."

Arriving at the end of the jungle they reached towards something that looked like a cave.

The entrance to the caves was framed by massive limestone formations weathered over the years into grotesque. Vines and creepers clung onto the entrance. A faint metallic scent hung in the air mixed with the earthy dampness. At the centre of the entrance, in an alien language was the name 'Caves of Atumkhor' inscribed. Deep carvings covered their surfaces, depicting strange symbols and humanoid figures which felt as if they were destroyed over time.

As they stepped inside, the temperature dropped noticeably, a chill wrapping around them like unseen fingers. The walls of the cave glistened with moisture, their surfaces embedded with tiny mineral deposits that shimmered under the beam of their flashlights. Stalactites and stalagmites loomed in irregular formations, some appearing as if frozen in the midst of reaching toward one another.

The cave from the within glowed with blue-green dim light even without the team switching on their headlamps. Strange bioluminescent fungi clung to the rough walls, casting ghostly shadows along the damp, uneven floor.

Anarina whispered, "It looks straight out of a movie or something I wish I saw in my dreams."

The team switched on their headlamps for a better view. The walls were alive with carvings. Unlike the weathered symbols outside, these were perfectly preserved, as if untouched by time. They depicted rows of humanoid figures kneeling before taller beings, their elongated skulls and piercing eyes eerily similar to the statues at the entrance. Some carvings showed festivities, while others illustrated sacrifices, figures being led to an altar, hands bound, as onlookers stood in rigid, solemn lines.

Exploring the cave from the within, Hills came across an inscription that felt repeated over and over again mentioning the importance of it. He called out to the others "Look, there is something carved in this cave repeatedly."

Hearing Hills, Anarina went to him with her notebook and pen to take a note of it. On decoding it she said "Alta Mina".

"What" asked Carrey.

"I don't know what it is, all that is mentioned is Alta Mina. no description, no information related to it is written on these walls."

Carrey stepped closer and looked at the drawings and carvings besides the words 'Alta Mina', her voice hushed. "What was Alta Mina? A kingdom? A civilization?"

Juno knelt beside another inscription, partially buried under dust and time. "Or a city," he added, "One that disappeared."

A little farther into the caves, the carvings depicted life in Alta Mina, a city with towering structures, bustling markets, and humans. Some frescoes showed celebrations, figures dressed in elaborate robes, carrying glowing objects toward an altar. Others took a darker turn: people in chains, sacrifices, and something even more disturbing; humanoid figures bowing before something not of this world.

In the center of the cave, a large circular platform sat slightly elevated, with a shallow pit in the middle. Rust-colored stains darkened the stone.

"A sacrificial altar," Juno muttered, his voice barely above a whisper.

The team exchanged uneasy glances. The cave wasn't just a place of worship, it had witnessed something much bigger, something tied to Alta Mina's fate.

Something that also caught all of their attention was a series of murals.

The first scene depicted Alta Mina, with towering spires, glowing courtyards, and intricate stone bridges. People of Alta Mina walked in harmony, their civilization thriving beneath celestial alignments.

At the center of the mural, two figures stood taller than the rest, dressed in ornate robes and a headdress of spiraling gold.

Pina and Alpina.

"Probably seems like the rulers of Alta Mina," Anarina whispered, tracing the carving with her fingers. "The leader of a civilization... and possibly the last of his kind."

In the next section of the mural, King Pina and Queen Alpina were seated on a grand throne, surrounded by the council. Below him, a group of people stood before an object; a small, smooth, metallic artifact, reflecting multiple hues of color.

Vela's breath hitched. "The Kabbot was in Alta Mina?"

The next part of the mural showed King Pina holding the Kabbot, his council watching as he received it from a tall, non-human figure. The being's features were faint, but its elongated head and slender frame were unmistakable.

"He didn't create it," Hills realized aloud. "It was given to him."

By whom? And for what purpose?

The final part of the mural gave no answers, only devastation.

The city was in flames—structures crumbling, people fleeing. Strange, shadowy beings loomed over them. The Kabbot, once held in reverence, was now being fought over.

At the very bottom, a final engraving stood alone.

Pina and Alpina running from the caves of Atumkhor, the Kabbot clutched in King Pina's hands.

While the team was still processing the mural, Anarina drifted her flashlight along the walls of the cave from one end to the other she gasped. "Everyone here".

The light through the flashlight revealed a massive celestial map spanning over a huge space probably about twenty feet wide.

It depicted a vast star system, the constellations marked with symbols that were not recognizable by anyone. A binary system where two suns orbiting each other was prominently displayed at the centre. Surrounding the twin stars were several planets, each carved with perfect fine detail.

The fourth planet from the larger sun, was circled and marked with the same insignia they had seen on the Pillars of Oynm.

"This isn't just a story, it's leading us to the unknown while also leaving us in suspense." Juno whispered.

Carrey stepped closer to see the binary system and gasped. "This binary system is beyond the Horsehead Nebula."

"Whoever built this city left these murals and drawings, knew very well about the deep space." Hills added.

Alta Mina had been a gateway to something far beyond Earth. And Pina Alpina had held the key, the Kabbot. A conclusion the team made in unison before moving ahead with their discovery.

Walking a little more deeper in the cave, they felt a low vibration. At first, it was faint, more like a distant tremor. Eventually it grew louder.

A deep humming sound resonated through the stone, vibrating beneath their feet.

It wasn't an echo.

It wasn't the wind.

Something was moving deep within the tunnels.

The team stood frozen.

Vela instantly without a second thought felt the Kabbot in her bag. It felt alive, almost breathing. The slight hums could be heard from the Kabbot as well, in sync with the hums of the caves. Vela grabbed it tight but eventually the hums from the Kabbot died out.

They wanted to get out of the cave but also not miss out on any piece of detail. Moving further into the darkness they saw nothing except their own light reflections.

As the sun dipped below the horizon, the ICMR members returned to the base camp. The camp was lit and the air smelled fresh because of the distant waves but a feeling of unease prevailed within the teams.

Lisa took charge and began, "Each team ventured deep into the island and had their own pieces of mysteries. But now it's time to piece together all these mysteries."

Team Research began with their part of findings. Rox dropped a collection of specimen jars and glowing plant samples onto the table. "This island isn't natural," he declared. "Some of these species shouldn't exist."

Jones unrolled his notes, shaking his head. "Some of the flora and fauna here have bioluminescence and electromagnetic responses that defy explanation."

Ted, the intern, tapped away on his laptop, his brows furrowed. "There's a pattern in their biology. It's almost like... something altered them."

Lisa, pressed her temples. "What do you mean?"

Jones exhaled. "I think this place—this entire island, was a controlled environment. A test site."

A long silence followed.

Eventually, to not waste any time further, Stones stood up and started, "We found something and that would change a lot of our perspectives about this island."

While Ed rolled out photographs, Juno said "Even we have something that was just not expected. But first let's hear what you have to say."

The images displayed crystallized structures, encased figures frozen mid-battle, faces contorted in expressions of rage and pain.

One image in particular sent a shiver through the group.

It was Sentori, a rebel commander, holding nearly 80% of the Kabbot in his grasp, just before being stabbed by Elara, the King's loyal warrior.

Tim took a deep breath. "This isn't just a ruin. It's a moment in time, frozen." He tapped one of his malfunctioning devices. "The magnetic field around the battlefield is still unstable, almost like something is holding time in place."

Ed, shifting uncomfortably, added, "And I know where the rest of the Kabbot is."

The group turned to him.

He hesitated, but then pointed at Vela, "The other part of the Kabbot... it's in her possession."

All the eyes were up on Vela. "How did you get it?" asked Juno.

"Before getting on the ship, I visited an antique shop and I found it there," she said in her defence.

"Nevermind, it will probably be of help." Stones exclaimed. "What did you all come across?"

Juno was the first to speak. "Crossing the pillars we came across a cave named 'Caves of Atumkhor'. The insides of the cave had a lot of hidden mysteries related to a city named 'Alta Mina'."

The team gathered as he unfurled a sketch and photographs of the cave murals; images of a grand civilization, ruled by Pina Alpina, thriving under unknown forces, then falling into chaos, consumed by war and destruction.

Anarina held up a photograph of a massive star map carved into the rock. "This is what we found in the caves."

Gasps rippled through the group as they recognized the celestial formations. The binary star system, the orbiting planets and the unmistakable outline of the Horsehead Nebula.

"Alta Mina wasn't just a lost city," Anarina said, her voice steady but filled with awe. "It was connected to something out there. And they knew about it before we even dreamed of space travel."

Hills stepped forward, his voice grim. "And then there's the Kabbot."

The camp fell silent.

Vela, still clutching her bag, hesitated before pulling out the silvery-grey object. Even in the dim firelight, its grooved surface shimmered, reflecting unseen colors.

"The Kabbot was given to Pina Alpina," she murmured, recalling the cave mural. "By someone, or something, not of this world."

Silence stretched between them as the realization sank in.

Then, from across the campfire, Ed finally spoke up, "We have to take it back to Suryl."

His voice was quiet but resolute. "Sentori had it when the battlefield froze. If we put the pieces together... maybe we'll understand what happened."

All the members were lost in thought.

Mr. Stones leaned forward. "Let's piece this together. We know that:

Alta Mina existed, and it was ruled by Pina Alpina.

The Kabbot was given to them by an unknown force.

Something destroyed them.

The Ruins of Suryl are frozen in time.

The Binary Map leads beyond Earth."

He looked at the group.

"But what we don't know is why."

The firelight flickered in Vela's eyes as she looked down at the Kabbot in her hands.

"We have to go back to the ruins," she said. "And we have to put the pieces of the Kabbot together."

"I don't think that would be a good idea." Emo said.

"But we would not be able to come to a conclusion without trying."

"Fine." Emo finally agreed.

Lisa nodded slowly. "Then it's settled."

The teams, though exhausted, knew that tonight was just the beginning.

Because whatever they had found here wasn't just a legend.

It was a warning.

Chapter 5

The Lost City of Alta Mina

The night was heavy with tension. The three teams had already spent hours piecing together their discoveries and findings related to the lost civilization and the artifact that would hold so much power that if in wrong hands could probably destroy everything.

There were various questions and the biggest one being 'what happened to Alta Mina?'

Lanterns flickered in the darkness and the team was getting ready to plan for the next day. Their journey would be back to the Ruins of Suryl the first thing in the morning. The discovery of the binary system and the horsehead nebula in the caves of Atumkhor was another site to be visited.

The secrets behind the ruins had to be revealed as it would lead them to the greater hidden secrets.

The night was getting darker and the hum of the insects grew louder in the silence. The members moved back to their tents, hopefully to have a goodnight sleep and wake up fresh for their next morning expedition.

The morning came upon and the members were ready for their trek to the ruins. The view had not changed one bit. The greenery and the flora and fauna was as alive as it could be. But what changed was their purpose to go to the ruins. This time it was not just exploration but to bring out the buried secrets.

★★

Tim once again glanced at his equipment just to see that the electromagnetic field was off the charts. As they crossed the pillars of Oynm, the whispers were once again heard. More like the wind was trying to talk to the pillars. The murmurs were beyond understanding but the voices were clear.

There were no words exchanged between the members as they walked towards the ruins.

The sight was as shocking as it had been the first time. The ruins stood silent beneath the heavy air of mystery, their jagged edges biting into the wind like the bones of a forgotten world. The team had gathered around the frozen battlefield, where crystalline structures encased warriors in a final moment of war, their expressions twisted in rage, pain, or unwavering defiance.

Vela ran her hand over the smooth, translucent surface of a frozen warrior. Beneath her fingertips, she could almost feel the echoes of the past; the clash of blades, the roars of battle, the desperate final moments before all fell silent. "This... it's unlike anything we've ever seen," she murmured, her breath clouding against the cold surface. The soldier within the crystal almost seemed like staring back at her as if provoking her. Her steps were retreating but her eyes were doing the exact opposite. She could not even blink until Ed who stood behind her gave her a slight nudge to get her eyes off the crystalized soldier. She turned back and looked at him. Her face was pale and could not believe what she had just seen, the sight ahead of her was impossible and unrealistic.

Ed whose eyes were also transfixed to the crystal before nudging Vela and breaking her free from the hypnotizing sight.

A towering man with chiseled features, his dark hair wild and frozen in mid-motion, eyes locked in a furious stare. His muscular arms gripped a fragmented metallic artifact, the Kabbot, as though protecting it with his final breath. A blade was driven deep into his abdomen, held by a second figure, a warrior whose expression was as fierce as it was sorrowful.

"This is them..." Ed whispered. "Sentori and Elara."

Sentori, a warrior of legend, a name that stirred both reverence and fear across the lands of Alta Mina. Standing at nearly seven feet tall, his presence alone had commanded armies. His body was sculpted with the scars of countless battles, his muscles hardened like stone. He had not been a mere soldier, he had been a visionary, a rebel leader who had sought to wield the Kabbot's power to reshape the world.

Whether his intentions had been noble or destructive was a debate that history never settled.

His armor, once golden and gleaming, was now tarnished with time, but the intricate patterns carved into the metal remained, ancient runes of protection and conquest. His dark eyes burned with an intensity that not even death had extinguished, and his battle-worn face carried an expression of defiance, as if still fighting an unseen war.

"Goddamn," Tim muttered as he studied the frozen warrior. "The guy looks like he could take on an entire army with his bare hands."

"He probably did," Lisa replied. She tapped at the inscriptions on his armor. "These markings... they're ceremonial. He wasn't just any soldier, he was a warlord."

"More than that," Anarina interjected, stepping closer. "Sentori was the chieftain of the rebellion against the monarchy of Alta Mina. He tried to claim the Kabbot, but history says he was... betrayed."

"By her," Vela whispered, motioning toward the second frozen figure.

Elara had been the blade of the monarchy, the shield of the people. Where Sentori embodied untamed strength, she was precision and discipline, a strategist whose every move was calculated. She had not sought war, but when it arrived, she had met it with unwavering resolve.

Her golden armor still shone, unmarred by time, hugging her lean, powerful frame. The insignia of Alta Mina's royal house was engraved onto her breastplate, marking her as the protector of the throne. A warrior sculpted by duty, she had sworn an oath to safeguard the kingdom at all costs.

Her hair, frozen in motion, streamed behind her like a battle flag. Her face, framed by the sharp angles of her jawline and high cheekbones, bore an expression of sorrow mingled with determination. Her blade was buried in Sentori's abdomen, and her free hand was outstretched, as if caught between striking a fatal blow and reaching for him in regret.

"She didn't want to kill him," Anarina observed, voice quiet with realization. "Look at her expression... she hesitated."

"Or she knew she had no choice," Jones muttered. "She was loyal to the King."

"She was loyal to something bigger than that," Stones corrected. "She was loyal to Alta Mina itself."

Vela exhaled sharply, stepping back. "This is more than just history... it's a warning."

Tim, who had been scanning the ruins with his malfunctioning equipment, turned. "A warning for what?"

Vela didn't answer. Instead, she reached into her pack, pulling out the fragmented half of the Kabbot. The metallic object, smooth yet organic, pulsed faintly as if aware of its missing piece. Ed caught the gleam in her eyes and nodded.

"We need to complete it." Ed said before leading Vela to the other piece of the artifact.

Emo once again hesitated, "I don't think it's a good idea, the Kabbot in Vela's hands is already pulsating, what if something even wrong happens?"

Vela almost agreed to what Emo said before looking back at the Kabbot in her hand and the other piece that was in Sentori's hands. "No, I think it would be better to take our chances and see what happens when we actually piece as a whole once again and see what happens next."

Ed agreed to what Vela just said. The others had a mixed opinion but before a unanimous decision could be made, Vela and Ed went forward towards the crystalized figure and pieced it as a whole.

Stones, a little frustrated, looked at Vela and Ed, "Why would you do that? The decision wasn't even taken yet and not everyone was convinced with the idea of piecing it together. What if something goes wrong? We are on an unknown island, before taking any step we have to discuss it with others and then go ahead with the plan."

Ed calm but straightforward with what he had to say, "We know that the decision was not taken and there might be adverse consequences we might face but until we take the risk we will not be able to bring out the secrets that this island holds. The crystal figures, binary system and Pina Alpina and how many more secrets we might come across and we might be able to find the truth for."

Agreeing to what Ed had just said Jones replied, "I think this is the right thing to do. It will bring us closer to what we are looking for."

With no other option left, the others as well agreed.

Vela once again touched the Kabbot to see if it actually felt alive or not. Instead of feeling any sort of pulsating sensation she could see visions. What she saw made her take a step back and tremble. The entire vision of the battle was in front of her eyes.

At first she felt an explosion of energy. Blinding white light shot through her veins. As soon as she felt that she jolted her hand away from the artifact. But then once again she put her hand over the Kabbot she felt the same sensation again but this time instead of retreating her hand back she felt that pain for a minute and then next she could see the entire vision of the battle between Sentori and Elara.

The sky, once a brilliant shade of crimson and gold, had been shattered by fire and smoke. Towering spires of pure gold, which once stood as symbols of Alta Mina's wisdom, now crumbled like brittle bones.

A storm of flames and battle cries engulfed the streets.

Vela stood in the heart of the war, but she was not herself. She was an observer, a ghost, caught between the tides of time. The battle raged around her, fierce and unrelenting. Warriors clad in ornate golden armor clashed with rebels donning crimson war paint, the metallic clang of blades ringing through the city like a death knell.

The air was thick with smoke and the scent of scorched stone.

At the center of it all, two warriors stood, locked in a deadly confrontation.

Sentori stood firm on his stance, his breath heavy and his form unbowed despite the wounds that bled across his chest and arms. His black war cloak now tattered and bloodied, billowed in the fierce wind that carried the cries of a dying city.

In his right hand was the Kabbot, gripped tightly. Its surface pulsing with luminescence almost as if alive. Its rainbow-like glow shimmered, its energies coiling like smoke in between Sentori's fingers. His determined gaze was laced with a fierceful exhaustion.

"The city was built on lies and it was never meant to stand." Sentori growled, his voice deep.

His long, raven-black hair clung to his sweat-drenched skin, strands falling into his piercing dark eyes, which burned with an emotion that could not be explained. His battle-worn bronze skin bore countless scars, each one a mark of his unyielding defiance against those who had once called him an outcast.

He raised the Kabbot high above his head, its glow intensifying.

"If I can't rule Alta Mina... then NO ONE WILL."

Lightning arced from the Kabbot, splitting the sky in half. The very air itself warped, the ground trembling beneath the weight of ancient power.

But before he could strike—

Elara appeared from the smoke, her blade gleaming with the light of the dying sun.

She moved with precision, her form blur as she leaped up and saved herself from Sentori's strike.

She was draped in battle armor, her golden breastplate bore the insignia of Alta Mina's lineage that bore the symbol of duty, honor and loyalty. Her dark amber eyes burned with fury.

"You have to stop this." Elara screamed with her grip tightening on the sword in her right hand.

Sentori ignored what Elara had to say and once again raised his sword to fight Elara but she protected herself well. Her sword gleamed under the sun and in one strike slashed Sentori's hand. The sword from his hand fell and his expression was switched over with agony.

The Kabbot in Sentori's right hand now fully activated sent shockwaves rippling through the battlefield. The city, already on the verge of ruins, began to collapse.

Elara gritted her teeth and lunged forward. The blades clashed. Amidst the collapse, the roar of the clashes could clearly be heard, the impact sending a blinding burst of golden sparks in the air. They danced between the light and shadow, trading blows that could end empires.

Sentori's strength was raw, brutal and unforgiving but Elara was faster, sharper and more precise.

She dodged his strike and drove her sword straight into his side.

Just then the Kabbot reacted to the fatal moment, unleashing a surge of energy. Waves of golden light exploded from its core, swallowing everything in its path.

Elara barely had time to pull out the sword from Sentori's side before their world turned white and more like crystals.

Just when they turned into crystals, Vela was brought back to reality.

She staggered backwards, gasping and her pulse quickened.

The ruins had returned, the battle long over, but the Kabbot was now glowing in Sentori's grip, no longer broken—whole.

Ed grabbed her shoulders, steadying her.

"What did you see?" he demanded.

Vela swallowed hard.

"The end of Alta Mina," she whispered. "The moment the Kabbot... destroyed everything."

Ed's fingers brushed against the Kabbot. Time fractured around him. The world twisted and bent, the ruins vanished as he was pulled into a different moment in the past.

He was another ghost witnessing the past.

The ground shook beneath Sentori's feet as he ran, his breath ragged and lungs burned. His boots slammed against the stone pathways, kicking up dust from the Alta Mina.

In his right hand the Kabbot pulsed wildly. Its energy coursing through his arm like lightning. It was alive. It was a force that could either reshape or destroy everything.

Behind him, Elara followed. He did not have to look back. He could feel her presence.

The path ahead turned into a wild, the streets giving way to thick jungle. Roots burst through the cracked ground and tangled vines clawing at his legs. Trees loomed overhead and their leaves glowed faintly in the darkness.

Soon Elara neared Sentori. A silver blade splashed past his shoulder, narrowly missing him. The air hissed as the tip of Elara's sword cut through his cloak. He twisted around, skidding to a stop.

Her golden armor was splattered with blood and dust, her chest rising and falling with heavy breaths. Her amber eyes were locked onto him, fierce but pained.

She raised her sword, pointing it at his chest. "Don't do this."

He gritted his teeth. "You're too late."

The Kabbot pulsed again in his grip, the glow intensifying.

Sentori felt its power, it was a living, breathing force, something older than the city itself.

He turned and sprinted towards the entrance of the cave of Atumkhor. The cave mouth open ahead, its walls in ancient carvings of rituals, sacrifices and celestial symbols.

Inside, the truth of Kabbot was awaiting him. But Elara wasn't done yet.

She lunged after him, her sword shining in the faint darkness.

She tackled him.

The impact sent them crashing onto the cold stone floor of the cave's entrance. The Kabbot skidded across the ground, landing just out of reach.

Sentori coughed, rolling onto his back, trying to push her off—

Elara's blade pressed against his throat.

The Kabbot pulsed and then everything went blank.

Ed was back in the present to the reality which was all a mystery.

His body jerked as he gasped for air.

Vela's face was the first thing he saw, her hands gripping his shoulders. "Ed! What the hell just happened?"

He sucked in a shaky breath.

"I... I saw it." He swallowed, his voice hoarse. "The night Alta Mina fell."

Lisa stepped closer. "What did you see?"

Ed exhaled. "Sentori stole the Kabbot. He ran to Atumkhor... Elara chased him." His eyes darkened, haunted. "She tried to stop him. But she was too late."

The team fell into stunned silence.

Then, Tim spoke, his voice low.

"What was in the cave?"

Ed looked back at the Kabbot, still clutched in Sentori's frozen grip.

As soon as **Anarina's** fingers brushed the Kabbot, a cold shiver ran down her spine. Her breath caught in her throat as a sudden wave of energy surged through her, pulling her consciousness into a world long lost to time.

The ruins vanished.

She stood within the Cave of Atumkhor, but it was no longer the place of dust, decay, and forgotten whispers that she had explored earlier. Instead, the walls were glowing, alive with pulsing alien symbols that shimmered as if whispering secrets to those who could understand them. Ancient murals covered every surface, depicting tall, elongated humanoid figures standing side by side with humans. Above them, symbols of two suns, a crescent moon, and constellations unknown to Earth shone with a celestial glow.

Then, the vision shifted.

Anarina stood in the middle of a grand festival. Banners of gold and crimson lined the streets, flickering under the glowing lanterns. Musicians played unfamiliar yet hypnotic melodies and people moved into a tranceful state. The tribes were dancing to the captivating rhythmic beats of OOOH, AAAH, and AAOOOH.... But what struck her was that aliens moved along with humans.

Towering figures with deep purple skin, their silver purple eyes reflective like gemstones, walked among the people of Alta Mina as equals. They wore flowing robes woven with celestial symbols, their movements slow, deliberate, as if they knew more than they spoke.

Then, as though the air itself had shifted, the celebration hushed.

A procession moved through the streets. Priests, their faces hidden behind intricate golden masks, carried a massive stone chest, and at the center of it all, King Pina and Queen Alpina—the rulers of Alta Mina, walked with solemn grace.

The vision twisted and the light dimmed. The laughter faded and the warm glow of lanterns was turned down.

It was no longer a place of joy.

The murals she had once admired were now stained with crimson, their vibrant images now twisted and smeared with chaos. The once-glowing inscriptions flickered, their energy dimmed, as though something had drained the life from them.

And in the center of the cavern, floating above an altar, was the Kabbot itself.

It pulsed like a beating heart, casting shadows against the walls.

Then, a pair of alien eyes emerged from the darkness.

Anarina tried to move, but she was frozen in place.

A deep, guttural voice whispered into her mind:

"The Kabbot was never meant for man."

A violent shockwave of energy exploded through her body, and just like that, she was thrown back into reality.

Stones realized that every person would see a different image when they touched a particular part of the Kabbot.

He reluctantly touched the Kabbot to see what the Kabbot would reveal to him.

At the center of it all, he saw two figures.

One was an alien, Rirun, tall and regal, his deep violet skin shimmering under the light of distant suns. His silver, piercing eyes reflected entire universes, his long fingers outstretched toward the object floating between them.

Opposite him stood a man, the King Pina clad in rich, ceremonial robes woven with the insignia of Alta Mina's royal house. A golden crown rested upon his brow, but his face held an unearthly glow, as though touched by something beyond human understanding.

Between them, the Kabbot floated, rotating slowly, whispering in languages not meant for mortals.

Rirun's voice thundered, his words carrying weight across the infinite void.

"This is not a gift. This is a burden."

Pina did not waver.

"It is our destiny."

The moment his fingers touched the Kabbot, light erupted from its core, swallowing everything.

Suddenly, **Stones** was no longer floating.

He was standing in the throne room of Alta Mina, watching Pina and Alpina kneel before an altar drenched in blood. King Pina's hands trembled as he held the Kabbot close to his chest, his face pale with fear.

Behind him, Rirun stood in silence, watching.

The alien spoke one final time, "You should never have taken it."

A blinding surge of golden light erupted, and Stones was thrown back into reality.

His hands trembled. His breath came in short gasps.

His voice was barely above a whisper, "The Kabbot wasn't given to man. It was stolen."

Jones hesitated as he placed his hand on the Kabbot, but the moment his fingers made contact, his mind was ripped away.

He found himself standing inside the Cave of Atumkhor, but it was no longer empty. Instead, it was filled with a crowd of chanting priests, their golden masks reflecting the flickering torchlight.

At the center of the cavern, a stone altar loomed high, covered in deep red stains. The scent of burning incense and something metallic—something like blood filled the air.

A group of men and women knelt before the altar, their heads bowed in submission.

Above them, hooded figures held ceremonial daggers, their edges gleaming under the torches.

Sacrifices.

Jones tried to move, to shout, to stop it but he was paralyzed, forced to witness what came next.

A sharp, final cry echoed through the cavern and Jones staggered back, his breath ragged and uneven, and suddenly—

The vision shattered. He was back. Back in the ruins.

His voice barely escaped his lips. "They didn't just worship the Kabbot... they fed it."

★★

All the members got back from their visit to the Ruins of Suryl. All of them had a pale and dull look on their faces after visualizing and hearing the various stories that a few saw.

"Let's relax a bit and get back out here in 30 minutes for a discussion." ordered Lisa.

All of them went back to their tents with their hearts racing and thoughts running in various directions all together.

A few relaxed, a few pondered over what had happened in the last few hours, but after about 25 minutes all of them started gathering at the centre of the base camp.

"Let's start, if everyone is here?" said Stones.

"Ok," replied Lisa and Juno in unison.

"So firstly let's map out this entire island now that we know about everything." suggested Tim.

"Makes sense," said Anarina.

"The island is about 60 square miles, filled with ancient ruins, dense jungles and towering hills with otherworldly flora and fauna that coexisted." started Emo.

"The base camp is 5 miles away from the shore and 3 miles away is the first pillar. The 7 pillars are exactly 50 metres away from each other. The thing about these pillars that is not normal are the whispers that begin and the malfunction of the devices due to the electromagnetic properties." said Tim.

Vela continued further, "To the left of the pillars is the Cave of Atumkhor 7 miles away. The trek there is rocky and uneven, a series of jagged hills, jungle where the vines spilled on the ground daring to trip you over. The entrance to the cave is covered in ancient carvings of sacrifices and an unknown binary system. A place where the Kabbot reacted."

"To the right of pillars 6 miles away is the ruins of Suryl. The path is equally dangerous. The ruin is a battlefield with crystallized formations of warriors where Sentori has the Kabbot in his right hand." said Ed.

"So further 5 miles away from the ruins is the castle. Strange whispers can be heard." A partially collapsed fortress, with grand staircases leading to throne rooms long abandoned. The air was thick with memories, the scent of incense still lingering as though time had not completely moved forward.

"So we have mapped the entire island out with the important concerns that were to be kept in mind. Is there anything missing according to anyone?" Lisa asked.

"No there is nothing as such that is left at least as of now." Carrey responded.

"But I think we should take help because this is not something we can solve alone." Jones suggested.

"I agree, I think taking the help of ASRA is necessary." suggested Stones.

"That's a good point and they would definitely be of better help." replied Anarina.

"Then it's final that tomorrow the first thing in the morning we connect to ASRA and ask them for help." Lisa concluded.

Chapter 6

Castle of Pina Alpina

The morning sun hung low over the ruins of Alta Mina, its golden light struggling to pierce through the lingering mist. The air was thick with the scent of damp earth and ancient stone, as if the past itself refused to be forgotten.

The events of the previous night had left the team with more questions than answers. Visions of the past. The fall of Alta Mina. The sacrifices. The betrayal. The war. Each revelation had only deepened the mystery.

Lisa, standing with her arms crossed, let out a slow breath. "So, we all agree?"

There was a moment of silence before Stones nodded. "We call ASRA."

The Archaeological Survey and Research Association (ASRA) was founded to investigate the forgotten civilizations buried beneath the sands and the artifacts that defied historical records. ASRA's mission had always been to uncover the impossible and make sense of the mysteries that history had ignored.

Over the years, ASRA had been secretly involved in expeditions across the world operating under government and private sponsorships. They had studied various strange anomalies, forgotten languages and the retrieved objects that modern science failed to explain.

But there was one thing ASRA had never been able to find—definitive proof of an ancient, pre-human alien influence on Earth.

There were two members from the ASRA team arriving; Mr. Win Brooks and Jen.

Mr. Brooks, an archaeologist, was a scholar when it came to science and archaeology. A tall, broad-shouldered man in his late forties, with a weathered face that carried the weight of the years spent in this field. His skin tanned and lined from the years spent in the sun and unforgiving climates. He had blue eyes, sharp and calculating, always searching for hidden truths. He was dressed in a sturdy field jacket and carried himself with confidence that came from years of experience. His voice, deep and steady. A kind that could silence an entire room.

Jen, the other member, in her mid-forties with an angular face and high cheekbones that made her look serious. Her skin was fair but sun-worn, a testament to long expeditions. Her dark brown eyes, always assessing, always skeptical as if perpetually searching for the weak line in a puzzle. Her hair was shoulder-length, jet black with a few strands of gray, usually tied back in a tight ponytail—functional, no-nonsense, just like the rest of her. She wore a fitted tactical vest over a long-sleeved dark gray shirt, cargo pants, and boots built for survival, not style.

Brooks and Jen arrived soon after the call was made. They reached the base camp just before noon. The island did not give them a welcoming vibe, it felt as if something was telling them a lot of secrets are buried which they might come across. There was an eerie sound they could hear.

As Brooks approached, Lisa stepped forward to greet him. "Mr. Brooks, thank you for coming."

Brooks gave a small nod, his eyes sweeping over the ruins. "You said it was urgent." His deep voice carried the weight of experience, but there was something else there, a hint of anticipation.

"It is," Stones interjected. "We've found something... something that doesn't belong in this time."

Brooks raised an eyebrow. "You'll have to be more specific."

Lisa exchanged glances with the team before motioning for them to follow. "Come with us. You're going to want to see this for yourself."

"Is there something about this island that feels off, or is it just me getting that sort of a feeling?" enquired Brooks.

"No, it has a vibe that will not feel welcoming. A lot about this island is just a secret to everyone until they actually go within and explore it." Lisa reassured.

"Alright then why don't you give us a brief about the island as we move forward," suggested Brooks.

Stones started with the few details about the island that they had come across in the past few days.

As they reached the seven pillars, they took a halt to show the carvings and make them hear the whispers. Brooks and Jen both exchanged confused glances when they could not decipher what the whispers were. Just like ICMR, even

ASRA was not sure what the pillars tried to say, was it perhaps a warning for all of them, they wondered. They were even informed of the malfunctioning of the devices because of the electromagnetic fluctuations.

Around the pillars they noticed the flora and the fauna. It was not normal. They glowed even during the day even though it was faint but its glow could not be mistaken. They could hear slight hums from the insects present around them. But what was even more surprising was that it was not just from the insects but also from the non-living objects.

Their silent glances exchanged all the unsaid words they could not say aloud.

"Let's move forward, there is something that would leave you in awe and make you wonder if science even exists or not." Lisa said.

The ruins of Suryl stretched before them, a history, and a war frozen in time. As Brooks and Jen followed Lisa and the rest inside the shattered remains of what had once been a part of a grand city was nothing more than just a battlefield turned into a graveyard with crystallized warriors. It felt as if the ruins were watching them, listening to them and also waiting to slowly reveal itself to the others.

The air was thick with the scent of aged stone mixed with something old like metallic that lingered. It was as if the ruins still held onto the echoes of the past, refusing to let them slip away completely.

The scene before them was beyond anything they had ever seen or encountered. The expressions of the warriors locked in an eternal struggle and rage, and the weapons frozen mid-air.

Brooks stopped walking for a moment as his sharp blue eyes scanned the entire landscape. His years of experience told him that this was no ordinary ruin. He had walked through the lost temples of the Amazon, stood among the remains of the forgotten civilizations buried under desert sands, but this... this was completely different than anything he had witnessed before.

He turned towards Lisa, "Tell me everything you know about this place."

Lisa exhaled and replied,"The ruins of Suryl mark the site of the final battle. This is where Sentori and Elara faced each other and also the exact place where time stopped."

Jen crossed her arms, "Stopped?" she repeated, her tone skeptical. "You mean metaphorically, right?" she asked as if she was just pranked by the ICMR.

Stones, with a serious look on his face as if stating the fact this is not a prank, shook his head, "No, literally. Look around you."

They all turned around, their eyes taking in the scene before them, the picture where everything was frozen for centuries probably.

The ruins were littered with crystal encased warriors, their expressions full of rage, pain and defiance. Some had swords hung in the mid-air, their weapons caught just before striking an enemy, few fallen to their knees and hands still reaching for weapons they would never lift again.

Lisa motioned towards the centre of the battlefield.

"This is what we wanted to show you."

In the middle of the battlefield were Sentori and Elara locked.

Sentori, a towering warrior, his muscular frame rigid with defiance, his right hand locked around the Kabbot. Though frozen, his expression remained one of raw determination, as if even death could not bring him to stop himself from doing something that would destroy everything. His dark eyes seemed to burn with a fire that had not yet been extinguished.

Elara stood before him, her golden armor gleaming beneath the layers of dust and time, her blade buried in his abdomen. Her face was caught in a moment of duty, her lips parted as if she wanted to speak before time had robbed her.

Brooks stepped forward, the stones beneath his foot crunching. Jen was almost in a state of shock, and her mouth wide open. "What is this? Is this even real?"

"We had the same reaction. Even we couldn't comprehend anything at first. The question and feeling, both, lingered as to how can humans be crystallized and how can they be stopped in time. This is clearly not making any sense but then again we noticed the other happenings on this island and realised nothing on this island is normal. It defies some or the other property or law of science." Lisa said.

"So how about now? Did you get an answer to your questions?" Brooks asked.

Stones let out a small sigh, "A bit of our questions were answered or probably we became even more confused after getting the answers to our questions. It is the Kabbot that led us to a conclusion that there is something about the island that is giving a warning as if something bad has already happened or it will happen."

"What do you mean?" Jen asked immediately as she forgot to breathe for a second.

Lisa hesitated and exchanged glances with the team before telling them about the Kabbot.

"Kabbot is a device that was broken and a part of it was already in Sentori's grip and the second part was found by Vela earlier which she got here. The other part that was with Vela pulsed sometimes as if it was almost alive. We decided to get both the parts together and see what would happen further."

"What happened after fixing both the parts together?" Jen asked before Lisa could finish.

Stones took over and completed. "The Kabbot shows scenes. It shows the memories and visuals of the past, the fall of Alta Mina, the war, the rituals, the sacrifices, and-"

"And, what?" impatiently Brooks asked.

"And the fact that the Kabbot wasn't given to the humans, it was stolen." Lisa said.

Listening to this, Brooks curiously kept his hand over the Kabbot to know more about the Kabbot as well as Alta Mina. The moment **Brooks'** fingers brushed the Kabbot, a shockwave of energy surged through his body, seizing his mind in an iron grip. The ruins vanished and what he could see was the path. The path leading to what was yet to be uncovered.

The air was filled with fog, he could smell the burning wood. He could see a beautiful pathway which led to someplace in the deep forest, at least that was what he assumed. The flowers blossomed and the leaves glowed brightly in the night.

The view was as beautiful as ever. There could not be something prettier than what he had seen in that moment. A narrow path filled with greenery and flora on its either side made the walk worthwhile. Sounds of birds chirping and the insects humming could be heard from among the trees and plants.

He was just about to figure out what the path was leading him to. And in a second, the entire view was changed. Brooks found himself in a completely different place.

He found himself standing before a massive archway, its golden letters inscribed with a name, 'Alta Mina'.

Beyond the arch stretched a road leading to a majestic palace gleaming under the sun. The air carried the soft scent of the flowers and gentle streams of crystal-clear water ran alongside the path. Birds with shimmering feathers soared through the sky, their songs blending harmoniously with the whispering wind.

The marbled palace loomed in the distance, its gold-plated domes catching the light. Water from the fountains danced in the palace courtyard, and the staircases were decorated with intricate carvings. Inside, the king and the queen sat upon their thrones, their jewel crowns shimmering brightly in the entire room. A council of ministers stood before them discussing the affairs of the kingdom. Among them sat mysterious otherworldly figures, looking more like aliens, tall beings with luminous skin and piercing violet eyes.

A sudden chill swept through the air. The golden glow of the palace flickered and a deep rumbling echoed. The world around Brooks trembled violently and the vision shattered like a fragile glass.

Brooks gasped and staggered backwards as the vision vanished and he was brought back to reality. He was once again standing in the ruins, the vision around him blurred for a second and then ahead of him saw the members of ICMR and Jen.

He took a hesitant step forward towards the Kabbot and looked at it for a minute or so as if it would change its appearance.

He tightened his grip around the Kabbot making everyone else glance at him.

Stones went forward and put his hand over Brooks' shoulders, "What are you trying to do and what was the vision that you saw?"

Brooks turned towards him, his face pale, "There is a palace ahead about five miles away from the ruins. It is no ordinary palace. It is a beautiful marbled palace, with water parks and fountains, there are 76 chambers and no chamber is the same, each has a unique quality or an aspect. There are exquisite antique items in the palace that didn't even fit in that time. The most shocking part about the palace and the vision that I just saw was the king and the queen sitting in the courtyard and with them were the council of ministers along with the aliens. There is something about the palace that we have to get close to. It has something related to Pina and Alpina which is in the end connected to the aliens and the Kabbot. It will reveal something that would be of great help to us and it is definitely trying to bring us close to finding out the truth."

"But then why are you trying to remove the Kabbot?" Lisa asked.

"The Kabbot is the main element that is connecting this island and bringing us to every secret that it is hiding so well. What would happen if the entire Kabbot is out of Sentori's hands, we don't know but we will have to find that by removing it and taking our chances. Kabbot always pulses when near the Ruins or the cave, so there is a chance that it might react when near the palace as well."

"You are right, but what if removing the Kabbot would lead to other adverse consequences?"

"We won't know that until we take our chances."

"Fine, let's give it a try."

It was difficult to get the Kabbot out of Sentori's hand but after a great deal of effort, he managed to get it out. He glanced at the others standing there along with him and then looked towards the exit which led to a path supposedly towards the palace.

They made their way to the exit. It was exactly like the one Brooks had visioned. A beautiful path, glowing flora and fauna, and the insects and birds humming. It almost felt like a dream. They momentarily forgot about all the ongoing drama they had been witnessing for the past few days and were lost in the beauty of the unnatural nature they had been close to.

Soon that beauty was replaced with a long trek, the landscape growing harsher as they moved up towards the interior of the island towards the palace.

There were massive rock formations, their surfaces worn smooth by centuries of wind and rain. They came across a few rocks with human skulls & skeletal remains which made them even more curious. The trek was tiring after crossing the beautiful patch of the jungle. The hill became steeper making it difficult for the two teams to even walk. From a distance, they could see an ancient structure. Nearing it, they came across the palace that looked nothing like it was in Brooks' vision. It had lost the charm that it had centuries ago and the beauty had faded into the ruins and the time that had passed.

"Are you sure this is the palace that you had visioned?" Juno asked with a tone of doubt.

"It is exactly what I had envisioned. The fountains and a massive backyard. A grand palace all in all." Brooks reassured Juno.

"Let's go in, we might find something else." Anarina suggested.

As they stepped in an eerie silence filled the air. The palace that was once grand and majestic is now nothing but a fractured remnant of the past. The scent of ancient decay and dust was in the air. The golden doors of the palace now nothing but tarnished and weathered remain.

Emo shivered as she gazed around, "The way the air shifts, it's like the past is breaking down our necks."

Jen warned everyone, "Stay close. This place is huge and completely unknown to us. We have to be careful and be with each other and not leave anyone behind."

Inside, the hallways now had cracked walls with spider webs hanging around. The grand courtroom was now filled with silent shouts and cries. The chandeliers lay fallen on the ground shattered across the floor. They could hear the echoes of their own footsteps.

The most haunting sight in the council chamber was the ghostly silhouettes of the past. The thought that the king, queen, the council of ministers and the aliens all sat together in that very chamber was a haunting thought and a sight as well. A strange hum could be heard in the chamber but nothing could be seen. The members could feel it, a vibe that did not settle well with them.

A sudden gust of wind howled through the chambers and whispered, "You should not have come here."

"Who said that?" asked Tim, "Stop pranking guys, it's not the time to joke."

"No one from us would do anything like that, especially not during a time like this when everyone is scared of what's going to happen next." Juno said calmly.

They paused for a moment and suddenly they heard the noise of water dripping from some distant place. They started walking towards the noise of water dripping and as they grew closer to it, the echoes grew louder and then at one point the noise was completely gone. Nothing could be heard apart from the echoes of their footsteps and their own voices.

They once again walked towards the courtroom and this time it was not just their hallucinations but the reality of the king and queen being seated in their respective thrones. Their shadows flickering in the darkness present in that room.

"What we are looking at, right in front of us, is this real?" Vela shivered.

"It sure is not a dream. But how is something like this even possible?" Ed replied.

Brooks took a step forward towards the thrones of the king and the queen and just when he was about to ask a question, the shadows vanished. All their faces had a look of shock. But before that they saw the king, Pina pointing his finger towards a door in the corner of the room.

The moment they saw the king point his finger towards the door, the Kabbot in Brooks' hand pulsed, it felt as if it was almost alive. The glow of the Kabbot deepened and its energy crackled with great intensity. The next moment all he could see was another visual.

Instead of the beauties of the palace, he saw the palace central hall filled with the king, queen and the other warriors around.

Amidst all of them were the aliens. They were in some sort of an urgent meeting at least that was what could have been interpreted.

"What do you want from us?" asked the king.

"We want Alta Mina," one of the aliens said firmly.

That was the only conversation he could hear from the central hall.

The next moment he was outside the palace. A path that would lead them to the palace. At first everything seemed to be normal. People moving here and there, bargaining for their purchases. Sellers' cries could be heard above all the other chatter. The marketplace was filled with clutter and daily chaos.

But as he moved forward, a little more nearer to the palace, he saw something that was disturbing and traumatizing.

Hundreds of people were enslaved, their backs bleeding from the continuous torture they were facing. Their arms scarred with the marks of the merciless whips of the armoured soldiers. Many were forced to kneel in front of the warriors of authority as they lashed their whips and in between those lashes their echoing laughter could be heard. Many were forced to do the labour work given to them, dragging massive stone blocks being one of the most exhausting works. Their bodies were being dragged with exhaustion as if they were almost dead bodies.

One of the slaves, an old frail man, collapsed to the ground right in front of Brooks' eyes. His body was too weak to even move a little.

The soldier whips the old man, “So you want freedom, here taste this, to the chagrin of other soldiers, the old man replied, cannot expect freedom from slaves, to which the soldier flogs him harder.”

Brooks flinched, all of this happening right in front of his sight but yet he could not do anything. The feeling of helplessness crept in with fear and sorrow clearly visible in his eyes.

A sudden siren rang through the air. The crowd, shouts and the cries were all momentarily silent. It felt as if there was a sudden change and no one else existed apart from Brooks. And the next moment, he was outside the palace.

The massive gates to the palace swung open revealing the way to the Central Hall. Brooks walked forward towards the hall, stepping over the pristine marble floor. The hall was grand, beyond one’s imagination. The pillars were massive and each had something engraved on it. Many had some celestial symbols, just like the ones found in the Caves of Atumkhor. Golden chandeliers lit the entire chamber with a warm, radiant glow.

At the far end, upon the thrones were seated king Pina and queen Alpina. Their faces were stern and they were dressed in jewels with their crowns glistening under the light. Around them, the soldiers stood in their armour. The otherworldly beings, the aliens stood out amongst all. Their tall, purple skinned figures with glistening violet eyes looked almost hypnotising.

One of them, his deep purple robe adorned with the same celestial symbols, raised his elongated finger and in an accent almost not understandable spoke, “Everyone must gather at the Caniula on time.”

Brooks lost in his thoughts and whispered to himself. The word 'Caniula' echoed in his mind.

Just then the alien directly looked towards Brooks. His gaze pierced and suddenly, Brooks was back in reality. His breath uneven, forehead full of sweat and head spiralling. He could not get a grip on himself. He almost felt dizzy.

The team around him looked at him with concern. After a minute or two of settling down, Stones asked, "Are you fine? What did you see? You just suddenly froze and then were suddenly brought back and you started gasping.

What happened?"

"I saw it," he said, almost frightened from the visuals. "The Alta Mina, before its fall. The people, the palace, King Pina, Queen Alpina, soldiers or the warriors, the aliens and something known as the Caniula."

"The what?" asked Anarina.

"Caniula." He repeated.

"What is that?" Jen asked.

"I don't know exactly. But from what I know it's a place where the aliens gather. We will have to figure the rest ourselves." Brooks replied. "But I did see the path to the Caniula in the vision. If we follow that we will reach it until something has been messed up again."

"Then let's go and search what we can get from there." Stones said adamantly.

"Fine. So first things first, the Caniula is about 1 mile away from the castle. The route is pretty much the same, rough terrain with vines and roots getting in the way, wanting to trip you over so be careful. And nothing about the view is beautiful anymore." Brooks warned everyone.

The already dull faces grew even more dull on listening to what Brooks had to say. The only good thing about this island was the view and the way it attracted them but now even that was not the case.

They began their journey towards the Caniula. As Brooks had already mentioned, nothing about the view was extraordinary.

They reached an open structure. As they entered, a wave of stale, dust laden air rushed past the group, carrying with it the scent of ancient stone and forgotten battles. The hallway beyond was lined with faded murals, depicting scenes of wars, alien envoys in deep discussion and grand festivities that once took place in that space.

Brooks stepped forward, his pulse quickening as the corridor opened in a massive, open-air amphitheatre. "This is the Caniula," Brooks whispered.

The amphitheatre was huge, its circular tiers of seating carved directly from polished white marble. Each row of seats descended towards the center, forming a coliseum-like arena. The central stage was an enormous flat stone platform, stitched with mystical symbols that seemed to faintly glow in the darkness. This was the place where the aliens had their meetings and conferences, the place of honour where the wrestlers fought and clashed against each other, and various sports events and competitions took place. There were a few chambers along the curved walls, used as waiting halls, weapon storage rooms and meeting quarters for the royals and aliens. The energy of the Caniula back in those days was unimaginable.

The Caniula was an open amphitheatre that would reveal the uncountable stars shining in the sky high above. Even after the number of years that had passed the Caniula still stood majestic just like how Brooks had visualised in the vision he viewed a few hours back.

But what caught Brooks' eyes was the stone carvings on the upper part of the walls of the amphitheatre. There were alien figures, their elongated forms intertwined with humans in depictions of knowledge-sharing, alliances and warnings. There were words and phrases written in an unknown ancient language.

Carrey exclaimed, "This place... It's more than just an arena or a battlefield. A place where the fate of many was decided."

"Yeah, something about this Caniula is weird, probably it is the vibe that I am getting from this place." Tim shot back.

A cold gust of wind swept through the open amphitheatre as the teams of ICMR and ASRA stood in silence, viewing the huge Caniula.

"This seems like the heart of Alta Mina." Carrey whispered.

Brooks instinctively tightened his grip on the Kabbot, its glow growing stronger with the pulsating feeling. He felt it pulling him towards something. It was definitely not towards the centre of the Caniula. He walked towards the pull only to find a hidden secret. His footsteps guided him to a large platform at the edge of the arena. The ground beneath was slightly uneven.

"That's not normal." Juno narrowed his eyes.

He knelt, brushing the dust away, revealing a faintly glowing symbol. Before anyone could react, the Kabbot pulsed violently with a deep mechanical rumble. The ground beneath them trembled.

The massive stone platform began to shift, rotating with a grinding sound as ancient mechanisms awakened after centuries. Dust and debris tumbled into the abyss as a hidden passage slowly revealed a spiraling staircase leading somewhere deep below the Caniula.

"What on earth is this?" Jones cautiously stepped back.

Vela's breath caught in her throat, "Please, tell me there is nothing weird buried under this. The island has already surprised us enough. I can't handle anymore surprises."

Brooks slowly exhaled, "There is just one way to find that."

Not speaking any further, he stepped towards the spiraling staircase with others following him reluctantly. The descent from the Caniula to the Calendula was long, the air growing thick with each step forward. The wall was filled with strange drawings. The energy emitted from the Kabbot pulsated louder, almost making it feel alive in the silence.

Finally they reached the bottom of the structure where the space suddenly opened up into something far beyond imagination.

They stood at the entrance of Calendula, viewing the massive, circular dome-shaped structure, its size equivalent to a football field. The walls hummed with an unknown energy, lined with alien glyphs and panels filled with pulsating lights. The technology around the dome looked completely from a different time, something that couldn't exist even a hundred years back.

At the centre of the chamber, a metallic deck loomed, holding a towering beamer like structure that emitted a faint glow. Around the room, a soft blue light glowed, giving a better view to the intricate patterns.

On the right, a bus-sized polyhedral reactor sat upon the platform, tubes and conduits snaking outward from its core.

"This sure is alien, in both literal and figurative meaning." Ed said trying to make the environment a little light, though that did not work very well.

Tim continued further, "This is nothing less than a movie. It's a combination of thriller, science and what not is left to witness further."

"Probably some romance as well." Lisa whispered hoping no one heard that.

On the far side of the chamber, a large enclosed structure stood apart from the rest, its walls lined with unknown symbols. At the top of the chamber, a massive display screen flickered to life.

It was in a language no one understood. Within those sentences two words stood completely apart from the rest. On decoding them Anarina called out, "Satian Hub."

The moment those words were called out from Anarina's lips, the display flickered violently and a distorted alien face appeared, its violet eyes piercing and expression absolutely unreadable.

"You should not have been here," was the only thing the alien spoke before the display shut off again completely.

"I don't think we should be here for long." Jen said with a shaky voice.

Brooks was still not convinced and hesitated but he had no other option apart from agreeing to what Jen said. Finding the roots of all the happenings was necessary but the safety of the others was a bigger priority.

A low mechanical sound was heard, as if something was activated, from a distant corner of the dome.

"We're done. We have to leave right now, before we are trapped in this place." Ed feared.

The team ran up the Calendula, returned back to the Caniula and in the darkness made their way towards the ruins. The faint glow from the flora and fauna nearby made them sigh in relief. One thing on that island that made them comfortable was the bioluminescence.

The team returned to the base camp, and the first task that was at hand was to light up the camp and settle down to discuss all the happenings that were witnessed.

Lisa stepped forward, "Let us break down everything into smaller fragments that would make it easier for us to calculate our next move."

Brooks gave a breakdown for the entire day, "We explored the ruins, where I took the Kabbot from Sentori and witnessed visions of Alta mina, a time when humans and aliens coexisted. Following its pull, we reached the Caniula, an open-air amphitheater, where the Kabbot's energy surged. It then led us deeper to the Calendula, a vast alien tech complex filled with advanced machinery. At the Satian Hub, a digital screen flickered on, revealing an alien figure that issued a chilling warning: "'You should not have come here.'"

"What is the next step, any suggestions?" Lisa asked as she noted down the details.

"We need to call in specialists, send an urgent request to the United Global Space Agency (UGSA). This is much bigger than what we were expecting." Stones replied with a tone of urgency.

"I too agree with him." Brooks added.

"Then let's go ahead with this decision. Tomorrow morning we will call them and ask them to send a team as soon as possible." Lisa confirmed.

After the decision was taken, the team sat under the starlit sky. No words were exchanged. The silence brought them solace, and that solace was enjoyed by all after an eventful day.

Chapter 7

The Satian Hub

The night was peaceful, as the tiredness crept in. No one thought about the various happenings and were fast asleep. The next morning came with a rising bright sun along with a little laziness. The past few eventful days had caused them to have a relaxing morning until the UGSA team arrived.

The first thing, after waking up, Lisa called the UGSA to ask them to send some help over to the island.

The tension at the base camp slowly grew as the team from UGSA arrived. They were already given a brief of the Kabbot and the recent discoveries as soon as they reached, by the ICMR and the ASRA.

UGSA, an elite scientific and exploration division dedicated to specially uncover extraterrestrial phenomena and advancing human knowledge of interstellar civilizations. The team that arrived at the island comprised three members, Max Carter, Olivia and Ean.

Max Carter, a project head and a seasoned exobiologist of UGSA. A man of logic and precision, is respected for his leadership under pressure, balancing scientific discovery with tactical awareness to ensure the team's safety. His sharp green eyes and broad shouldered commanding presence make him an intimidating figure.

Along with him, Olivia, his subordinate and second-in-command, a brilliant quantum physicist specialised in interstellar propulsion. A completely contradicting personality to that of Max, Olivia was driven by curiosity and ambition.

Ean, another member of the team, an enigmatic UGSA specialist. An absolute introvert who would hardly utter a word, but when he does there is no nonsense, only logic in his talks.

On the revelation of the Kabbot to the UGSA team, Max found it difficult to accept something like this actually happening until he held it in his hands and visualised a few bits and pieces of Alta Mina. On the contrary, Olivia's curiosity made her believe that understanding the technology of Alta Mina could be the scientific revolution. The advanced machinery served as a breakthrough in quantum physics.

Max adjusted the visor on his helmet, his gaze sharp ahead as he asked Brooks, "Alright, so there is something that you have found down there. So tell me what exactly have you found?"

Brooks exhaled and exchanged glances with Lisa and then he started, "We discovered an alien infrastructure beneath an open amphitheatre and what's even more shocking is that it is still intact and in a proper working condition as in operational."

"What do you mean by operational?" Olivia asked curiously without wasting even a second.

Lisa stepped forward, "We're talking about a fully functional technological chamber."

"Where exactly is this?"he asked as if everything they said was normal.

"It is called the Calendula, located beneath an open-amphitheatre, Caniula." Brooks informed.

"Calendula?" Olivia's interest piqued.

Stones nodded, "A massive underground alien facility. It is still power and still running. There are mushroom shaped domes, enormous data structures and a reactor polyhedral device that we couldn't even understand."

Max, slowly getting curious, asked sarcastically, "What about the Kabbot, the relic you found?"

Brooks hesitated then took out the Kabbot from his bag once again, "This was the device that got us here. Upon reaching here, we could not decode everything but two words stood apart from the rest. One of the members from the ICMR decoded those words and said 'Satian Hub' to which an alien appeared on the huge massive screen above and told us we should not have come here."

"So you are telling me that you saw a visual, where you were guided to the Caniula and then you discovered the Calendula and then an alien appears and tells you that it would have been better for you to not come here? Then why did the Kabbot have to show you such a visual?" asked Max.

"That's exactly something even we can't decipher." replied Lisa.

After getting the gist of the entire situation, Max folded his arms and said, "Fine. Olivia, let's get our scanners and other equipment ready and see what is there in that Calendula that is so surprising."

The UGSA team descended into the depths of history of Alta mina, the ruins, caves and the Caniula that led them to Calendula.

As they proceeded deeper into the Calendula, they followed the faint glow of the alien symbols etched onto the walls. The air grew cooler, charged with an unseen energy that could send a subtle shiver down the spine. As they reached the bottom, the corridor widened and opened into a massive dome shaped Calendula.

The mood within the chamber was overwhelming. The ceiling stretched high above them, illuminated by soft, pulsating neon-blue veins running across the curved walls. The entire structure was untouched and the alien machinery still operational. Unlike the entire island that felt as though it was dead except the glowing plants and animals, this place felt completely the opposite.

Ean took a slow step forward, "This isn't just an underground chamber, like you mentioned its completely powered and nothing that could've existed centuries ago."

At the centre of the complex, stood a circular deck elevated, surrounded by holographic projections of unknown celestial bodies. Everything seemed completely different from what the others had seen the other day. The deeper they entered the chamber, the more discoveries they were able to make. There were floating platforms, which seemed unaffected by gravity, hovered in perfect formation, pulsating with a faint light. There were enormous mushroom shaped domes, their metallic surfaces covered in intricate inscriptions. The designs were completely alien.

"Isn't this completely different from what we saw?" Stones turned towards Brooks.

"It is. It's as if the Calendula is trying to reveal something but it is not doing this all at once. As if it wants to show certain details only in front of some specific people."

To the left, a row of computers lined the walls, their interfaces flickering with alien symbols and readings. The machines were anything but nothing like a human could create. Its mechanical precision, its operation, processing and analyzing unseen data was way beyond human capabilities. Some streamed flashes of another galaxy, stars and unpredictable star maps, while others streamed coded messages. Olivia approached one of the terminals with her equipment, but was unable to decipher anything since the scanner could not read the language.

Olivia touched one of the terminals lightly, "These could be some sort of data storage units or energy conductors."

"Probably. But what is shocking is all of it yet working even without any maintenance throughout these years."

The most striking thing in the chamber was the colossal polyhedral structure that still remained in the exact position they had seen the previous day. It was almost the size of a transport bus, its dark metallic surface constantly shifting, changing into different geometric patterns as though responding to an unforeseen force. Its presence was commanding, and radiating a deep and resonant hum that reverberated throughout the chamber. A mix of expressions could be seen on the faces of everyone present in that chamber.

"What is that?" Max muttered.

"It looks like a Quantum Resonator. But the readings once again don't make any sense." Olivia said.

Max read the strange reactor, "If it is still active, then it means someone or something is controlling and maintaining it."

Stones glanced around, "It does not look like that. At least not looking at the chamber and the island as a whole as well."

"Thats true, but you never know. This island is definitely strange, so you don't know what to expect." Brooks replied, looking at Stones.

Beyond the resonator, at the far end, stood the Satian Hub, a raised command centre embedded into the complex wall. Above it a large screen flickered, static distorting its image. Ean, Max and Olivia, stood in awe of the Satian Hub and the screen above. By now the ICMR and the ASRA team were so used to the happenings that nothing shocked them any further.

The screen flickered on for a moment and in a second it was switched off again.

Ean stepped closer, "Someone seems to be controlling all of this."

The deeper they explored, the more they were exploring the past and walking straight towards something that was not meant for human eyes.

Max suddenly thought of the Kabbot. "Brooks, do you have the Kabbot with you right now as well?"

"I have it in my bag." Brooks replied not knowing what Max was thinking.

"Give it to me. If touching different parts of the Kabbot reveals something about the past, Alta Mina, the caves, ruins, Caniula, Calendula and what not, then if I touch the Kabbot even I would be able to see some visuals that would be of some help to us."

"Right." Brooks said removing the Kabbot.

The moment Brooks gave **Max** the Kabbot, and he held it tight in his hand, an invisible force pulled him. A sudden surge of energy was felt by him, flickering lights and distorted echoes were heard. The vision was right in front of him, he almost lived that visualization in reality except the fact, he was nothing but just an invisible force into the past.

He was no longer in the massive Caniula or the Calendula. Instead, he stood within a fully operational alien facility, its walls gleaming with energy. The air hummed with advanced machinery and strange holographic symbols danced across consoles made of a material that were far beyond human understanding and reach. The chamber was vast and multiple levels with each level fully functional with floating walkways suspended over luminous energy cores.

Max's pulse quickened as he realized where he was and what was in front of him.

The Satian Hub was fully functional and intact in its prime.

At the centre of the room, seated on a throne was a tall, imposing alien with piercing violet eyes and an intricate exosuit that glowed with energy pulses.

Max was not sure who he was, until he heard someone mention his name 'Rirun'.

Rirun's fingers, elongated, hovered over a floating holographic interface, streams of alien data beneath his touch. His expression was unreadable, cold, calculating but beneath it there was something deeper, something he tried to hide.

A deep voice filled the chamber. "We need more human stock."

Max turned towards the sound of the voice.

Standing behind Max and opposite Rirun was another figure, tall and more commanding, his dark robes flowing like liquid metal. His violet eyes gleamed under light.

"Isn't this much enough, Oryx?" Rirun asked.

"Oryx" Max thought to himself.

Oryx inclined his head slightly, "No. We need more. The extractions have begun and the process is already in motion."

Max's tension heightened. "Extractions, human stock? Process? What are they talking about?"

Oryx further continued and warned Rirun, "Make sure that the shipments remain as a top secret and no one should be aware of it."

"Got it." Rirun replied.

Max's mind reeled. He did not know what was going on and what these visuals were trying to convey. He tried to follow Rirun's movements as the alien adjusted a few settings but learned nothing from the distance. He could not move any closer to Rirun since he was in the past. Suddenly, a detailed star map appeared, but it wasn't Alta Mina. Instead it was the Earth.

Max was cold, he went blank and was completely clueless how to respond to the entire vision in front of his eyes.

Oryx slightly turned towards Rirun, "The fate of Alta Mina depends on the completion of the cycle."

"What cycle were they talking about?" Max thought to himself.

Rirun's hand ran over a console, a massive machine in the room hummed to life.

The sound of the machine was loud which forced Max to turn towards it.

It was a beamer. A towering device which was activated and its core vibrating with a deep energy pulse, sending a golden arc of light that stretched from the ground to the ceiling. Within a few moments, a silvery semi-transparent substance rose from the chamber and was transported upward.

Max tried to take a step forward, to see what the substance was or where it was headed, but he could not even move an inch ahead.

Rirun's voice came through once again, "The cycle must be completed. Alta Mina must endure-", before he could have completed the sentence, Max was shuddered back to reality. A blinding white light engulfed him.

The moment he was brought back to reality, he panicked. He gasped violently and his body staggered backwards. The Kabbot in his hands involuntarily fell, making a thundering noise across the chamber. He nearly fell to his knees.

Everyone around him was shocked. Others who had viewed visions never had a similar impact on them. This was different.

From Max's behaviour they could tell, he viewed too much, something that a human could not take in all at once.

"Max", Olivia held him by his arm. "What happened? Are you alright?"

Stones sensing the fact that Max wasn't yet in the zone to speak, "It's the impact of the visual. He must've seen something that would be really disturbing. None of us who saw a vision reacted in such a way. There is definitely something related to this chamber that he saw."

After a few minutes of silence, Max was back conscious except for the fact that he looked extremely pale. "I saw them. I saw Oryx and Rirun."

"Oryx and Rirun, who are they?" asked Brooks, completely confused.

"Aliens. I heard them talking about extractions. And the most shocking thing I heard was that they take humans from earth, and use human extractions. What does that mean? I don't know. There was a huge machine, something like a beamer and from it some substance was being pulled."

"What sort of substance?"

"I don't know, but it is definitely something dangerous. Alta Mina wasn't just a civilization thriving in peace. Something was going on. Something we should have never known."

Max turned towards the Satian Hub, where he had witnessed Oryx and Rirun communicating with each other. His heart rate was quick, it felt as if his heart would jump out of his body. "This was where the Kabbot was originally."

His gaze locked on the panel. Without any word, he stepped forward, towards the final piece of the puzzle.

He was going to install the Kabbot.

His fingers hovered over the console, the air around them grew thicker and a low hum filled the chamber.

Above them the massive screen flickered and an image appeared in front of them.

It was Rirun. His violet eyes locked onto them and gave a stare as though he could break them with just a look in his eyes.

He then spoke with the same look in his eyes, "You should not be doing that." with just that being said the image in front of them vanished.

Max stood frozen in front of the console. The chamber hummed with energy, as if the walls could recognize the Kabbot's presence. He contemplated whether to install the artifact back into its place or not. After a moment of thinking, his hand made contact with the panel.

The pulsing blue veins running across the Calendula flared to life, their glow intensifying as the alien symbols rushed across the digital interfaces. A deep mechanical thud resonated throughout the chamber, vibrating a beat beneath their feet.

"Max, wait!" Olivia shouted but it was too late, she already missed her chance.

Max had already placed the Kabbot in its original place.

The minute the Kabbot was locked into its place, a blinding pulse started beating within the artifact. The team took a few steps back. Holographic interfaces came to life, projecting massive alien schematics, energy readings and celestial maps.

Above them the display flickered before stabilizing, revealing an image of Rirun. This wasn't just a recording above them, but real time.

Rirun could see them and they could see Rirun. This wasn't just another vision but a view they were watching in reality.

The alien's gaze narrowed and his expression unreadable. Then his voice in the chamber echoed, "You shouldn't have done that."

"Is that a recording?" Ean asked.

"Maybe, maybe not." Max replied.

"But how can any of this be possible? The Kabbot is ancient, the technology is ancient, but how can it all work yet- that too perfectly?" Olivia questioned.

Everyone gave a confused look to each other present there. Rirun's expression was neutral but his gaze shifted as though studying them. Then with a calm yet authoritative voice he said, "Identify yourselves."

Max hesitantly looked towards Olivia, since there was nothing he could do any further. He stepped closer to the console, directly talking to the alien.

"My name is Max Carter and we are from the UGSA, ICMR and the ASRA. We uncovered this island and now we want to know what exactly happened to this island. We have many questions in our minds and we want answers to all those questions."

Rirun tilted his head slightly. His fingers glowing, suddenly moved across an unseen console. The beamer at the centre of the chamber hummed to life. The massive device pulsed with a golden arc of light sending waves of energy through the room. His eyes darkened and in a rough voice said out aloud, "You are not the first and definitely not the last as well."

"What do you mean?" Brooks asked.

"You were never supposed to find any of this but now that you have, the cycle has begun again."

"What cycle are you talking-" before Ean could complete the sentence, the chamber shook violently. Warning symbols flashed across the alien screens and the resonance from the Quantum Resonator intensified.

Olivia with a face of frustration, "Max whatever you just did right now is going to cause a lot of trouble. It's sending a powerful transmission."

Max in turn blurted out almost a whisper, "I didn't know this would happen." He hoped no one heard him or else it could create a rift within the group at an extremely crucial moment.

Stones stepped up, "What is done is done so let's not argue about that right now. But the question is that if this is live then who is on the other end?"

The question was answered by just the entry of another alien, his presence imposing and he stood next to Rirun- his name Oryx. His gaze swept over them and then he spoke, his voice low filled with unmistakable authority, "More the trespassers, more the violations of the cycle."

Max with a refused look, "We're not trespassers, we're explorers and we're here to seek knowledge of this island and how it appeared on the map suddenly."

"Well none of it matters now." Oryx said. The ground below them trembled, the symbols on the wall started shifting and the beamer pulsed brighter with its golden glow intensifying.

Olivia's eyes widened with fear clearly visible, "I think this isn't just reacting but actually waking up."

"We need to shut this down. Probably try and remove the Kabbot once again from its place and see what happens." Ean suggested.

"You can't do that. The Kabbot cannot be removed again since it's back in its original place." Rirun replied before anyone could even try or say something.

Max, frustrated, asked, "Then explain to us everything, about the war, the caves, the Calendula."

"You'll know about it over a period of time." Rirun replied back.

And then once again the screen went blank. This confused every one even more, because the play in front of them was blurring the lines between the past and the present. A mechanical roar erupted within the Calendula from the Satian Hub. The beamer pulsed with energy, releasing a wave of energy, the entire chamber trembled. The Kabbot now fully linked to the system, started sending shockwaves through the alien infrastructure.

Lights flashed, alarms blared and something unfamiliar surged.

Max, frustrated, turned towards others, "We have to get out, Now."

Chapter 8

The Quantum Resonance

Silence filled the Calendula as Max pressed the Kabbot placed on the Satian Hub's control panel. For a few moments nothing happened and everything went back to how it was before the digital screen flickered on. The only thing they could hear was the sound of their own breathing.

And suddenly a deep hum vibrated through the chamber, as if the ancient machine had recognised the Kabbot's presence. The walls trembled and the energy they felt once again strong. The team once again stepped back.

Max hesitantly asked, "What if I press the Kabbot once again? Do you guys think this will stop?"

"I highly doubt that." Stones gave his opinion.

"No, don't do anything now. You've already brought to life the aliens and stuff." Olivia firmly said.

"But we won't know anything until we give it a try. And what's the most that will happen? Either way we're trapped in this, so might as well take all our chances and give all possibilities a try." Max said.

"I think this makes sense." Brooks' pointed out.

Before anyone else could react or respond, a sudden shockwave erupted, sending a rippling pulse of golden-white light across the room. Fear was clearly visible on their faces. In the fastest pace possible, Max ran over and pressed the Kabbot once again. The air crackled and the energy wave touched the surroundings, the alien terminals flared to life, flooding the chamber with an overwhelming cascade of symbols and data.

"I told you we shouldn't have done that. This is giving me a bad feeling." Olivia whispered.

The deep voice of the Satian Hub's system roared across the chamber, KABBOT IS LIVE.

"Satian Hub online."

"Primary systems activated."

"Quantum synchronization in progress." The words flew in the air as the atmosphere in the Satian Hub slowly changed.

"What the hell is happening?" Ean almost shouted.

Olivia's eyes widened as she glanced at the room filled with holographic projections. "This system is far more advanced than what we thought. These computations are currently active, it's like we've restarted an entire network once again." she pointed out to the spiralling alien codes.

Max remained tense, his gaze locked on the Kabbot. The artifact no longer remained an artifact but was now the beating heart of not just the Calendula but the entire Alta Mina. He thought about what Olivia had said before he pressed the

Kabbot once again. There was a slight look of regret on his face for not listening to Olivia, but at the same time felt it was necessary to do that to bring out the real truth of the Kabbot, the city and the secret it has been hiding.

Ean held his fist tight, almost ready to fight someone. "Great, now we have these computers, in fact the entire system working, but what exactly are they doing? Because if this thing is now alive, then we are most likely to be in huge trouble and I don't know how we are going to get out of this."

Olivia held her equipment and tried to decipher the alien data streaming in their surroundings. "This system is huge and massive. I don't think this is just some power plant or a control centre. This Calendula is something more than any of it, something like an intelligence hub, and we just reactivated the entire system."

"Then let's face it." Max said with a firm look.

"We anyways don't have a better option than doing that." Olivia spoke almost frustrated.

The holographic projections surrounding the hub shifted, their static screens now displaying a rapid succession of celestial images, structural schematics and energy readings.

The alien voice once again commanding, delivering a series of cryptic messages in an ancient dialect. The words could not be understood since they were not in English, but the Kabbot instantly reacted and translated into a language that could be understood by the others.

"Data link established."

"System diagnostic: 99% functional."

"Last command logged: cycle initiation."

Stones' breath was caught in his throat, "Cycle initiation?" He turned towards Max. "Is that the same thing you heard in the vision you viewed?"

"It is the same. But the thing is we still don't know anything about this so-called cycle and what it is referring to."

A sudden hum echoed through the facility. The ground beneath them trembled as the beamer, a towering alien structure began to activate. The golden arc of energy flared to life.

The team turned around, watching as the device began operating as if it had never been deactivated.

Olivia's beamer beeped, "Max there is something here, the beamer-", she couldn't even complete her entire sentence.

Everyone looked up at the massive machine, its energy readings were beyond human's understanding.

Above them the Satian hub display screen flickered. The entire Calendula roared to life. Screens that were dark now were switched on with alien symbols, million tiny lights igniting along the curved walls. A holographic projection of a vast, swirling galaxy emerged above them, the stars shined, planets orbiting at the centre and a binary system unlike anything recorded by human life.

The screen stabilized and a clearer image appeared, more precisely a planet. It was neither Alta Mina, nor Earth. Whatever it was, it was beautiful. A sky bathed in crimson blue, with colossal alien structures that almost towered towards heaven.

Beneath this view only one word displayed- 'El-Bon'.

"Is that another planet?" Ean questioned.

"Looks like that." Brooks replied.

"Let's first go back to the base camp and contact someone to get a better idea of all of this." Max suggested.

"Contact who?" Olivia questioned.

"That's not important right now. We first need to head back." Max answered.

"Fine." Olivia finally gave up the argument.

They ran out of the Calendula and the surroundings did look a little changed but their rush to get back to the base camp did not give them a second to look up and notice.

On reaching the base camp the five of them were bombarded with all sorts of questions and the only thing they could reply was,"We might be in danger, let us first talk to someone and get this sorted and then answer all the questions you guys have."

As soon as Max called his head from UGSA, he himself was answerable to many questions. He could not decipher what was happening. There were no answers that he had. He had called UGSA to get solutions but to his shock he himself was answerable. Something that was not in his hands made him go blank at least at that very moment.

Across the globe, every major observatory, radar station and scientific research facility detected an anomaly. The magnetic field of the earth was shaken. Satellites wobbled in their orbits. Radio signals as well were scrambled and their frequencies hijacked by some unknown source. People all around the world trembled.

A team of scientists panicked in a Space Observatory and stared in shock at their screens as the earth's magnetic poles shifted.

"What the hell is happening?" One of them shouted.

"We don't know. It seems like some alien force being exerted on the earth's core." Another one shouted.

In Tokyo, air traffic controllers screamed as the city's power grid fluctuated, causing panic at the airports. They went dark, subway systems screeched to a halt and skyscrapers flickered.

In the Atlantic Ocean, the Auroras, seen at the poles, began swirling at the equator. A sight never seen before, in fact never thought before. Their emerald and violet hues shimmered across the sky, mesmerizing and terrifying those witnessing it near the most unexpected place, Brazil and West Africa.

"What are we supposed to do? These are just a few places I am talking about, there are a lot more that I can name." The one on the other end shouted.

Max had no reply to that. "We were actually not aware of any of this. We just had to take our chances. But we did not know this would affect the entire earth as well."

"Well now it has. Do you have any solutions?"

"As of now, none. But we will come up with something. If there is something else that occurs there please keep us informed."

"Alright. Any solution you come up with needs to be discussed with me first and then implemented."

As soon as the call ended, he turned towards the rest of the group.

He looked frail. He sighed, "I called at the UGSA headquarters, but the information I was given was even more... I don't know how to put it in words. The Kabbot now fixed in the Satian Hub has caused even more problems not just here but also on earth. Before I could ask for a solution, I was notified with the information that the magnetic field on earth is shaken. They've asked us to come up with some solution and before we implement it we have to get permission from them and inform them of the solution. If they approve then we can put it into action."

Everyone stared at him as if they heard him speak some unknown language. He looked up at everyone, took a brief glance and his head hung low once again. Olivia's eyes were stuck on him. A look of anguish replaced all the stress over her face. But at the same time she knew blaming him would bring no good to anyone.

The air was thick and the sky dark. The sun was replaced with a beautifully glowing moon. All their faces were mirrored with nothing but tiredness. They all retired to their tents in their cozy sleeping bags. At least most of them. Max could not forget about the events that took place. The entire day was a mix of adventures and it was not just them but everyone on earth as well suffering. He never thought that the search for extra-terrestrial life and alien civilization would lead them right here on Earth.

Sitting by the bonfire, with his palms covering his face, he thought hard to come up with a solution and save everyone from whatever all of the mess that was created. Just then he felt a hand on his shoulder. He looked up to the owner of the hand and saw none other than Olivia. He was surprised to see her. Even after all this, she came to cheer him up.

"What are you doing here?" Max asked, trying hard not to bring tears in his eyes.

"That's the same question I could ask you."

"Ya, well I don't know. I should've listened to you when you told me not to put the Kabbot back in its place, but I just didn't listen to you. I don't know what will happen and where do I get a solution from."

"It's okay. You did not do that not on purpose. And as you said if we won't try we won't know. Any ways what is done is done, no point in brooding over it. So get up and rest, tomorrow is going to be a long day."

"Hmm. You are right."

"I am always right, and you can't even deny it." Olivia tried to lighten up the mood.

"Yeah, yeah as you say." He finally smiled.

Max let out a sigh of relief. They both walked to their respective tents, looked at each other, gave a warm smile and finally said goodnight.

The next day was going to be hectic and thinking about it gave him a headache. He buried his head in the inflatable pillow and shut his eyes.

The next morning brought no sort of relief. Their faces pale and drained, and eyes wanting more sleep. A mutual feeling between them all was that they wished the night did not end so soon and the fact that they could sleep a little more. They never missed their homes more than they ever did that morning.

A peaceful Sunday morning, the sun hitting their faces lightly through the curtains and a delicious breakfast on a lazy morning. But currently all of that was just something they wished came true. They were like kids waiting for some sort of magic to happen or wake them up from a dream that felt more like a nightmare.

After a cup of coffee and shaking their sleep away, they all got ready for another mysterious day. It was not just a new day, but a fresh opportunity to live & make a difference.

Max after a slight hesitation spoke up, "Let's visit the Satian Hub once again, we might get some other clue."

"Yeah, agreed. There are a lot of secrets in my opinion that the Satian Hub is holding and we need to get to it." Lisa added.

"Let us leave now then." Max said a little more confidently.

They all reached the Calendula. Those who saw the structure for the first time were awe-struck. They could not believe their eyes. They walked to the alien structure, the Satain Hub.

"Is this even real? I have not even seen this in the most advanced country and you guys are saying that this was centuries ago. Technology like this in those times is impossible to even imagine in your wildest dreams." Tim exclaimed.

"There is no point in being so shocked at this point. The island has already given plenty of chances to think how something like this even exists. But here we are." Stones remarked.

Everyone fell silent until they noticed an enormous holographic projection that was streaming real-time data. The alien machine began shifting and twisting like a sleeping beast waking up from deep slumber after centuries. None of it was from the past. It was in the present, 13 June 2047, in the exact same moment they were all breathing in.

"This is a recording or some sort of playback, right?" Anarina skeptically asked.

"No." a straightforward answer was given by Olivia.

"You've got to be kidding me. What in the world is all of this?" Lisa's eyes widened.

"The Kabbot is transmitting some energy I suppose," Brooks said, stepping closer to the Kabbot, "Something that is far beyond earth and human reach."

"The Kabbot?" Vela asked with shock painted all over her face.

Max walked towards the Kabbot, standing almost in line with Brooks. He trembled at the clear view of the Kabbot. Even the silence in that hub killed him from within. He felt responsible for all the happenings and his impulsive actions.

Olivia stood next to him and put her hand over his shoulder and gave him a reassuring smile with words hidden that everything is going to be alright, they are together in all the happenings and no one would hold him responsible. He nodded and gave her a smile back telling her he is fine. He gathered himself together, took a deep breath and convinced himself it's all alright.

Vela once again, was going to say something when suddenly the holographic projection zoomed in, the swirling galaxy narrowing its focus and drawing them closer and closer to the unknown binary system. The projection zoomed through the vast stretches of the deep, dark space until a single alien world was in the view, an Earth-sized planet bathed in the twin light of two suns.

As if the machines could understand the confused faces of all the members present in the room, the screen flashed with a name, 'El-Bon'.

The landscape unfolded before them and the view was something absolutely unseen. Towering mushroom-like structures, jutted from the ground like twisted monoliths, their surface reflecting the light of the twin suns. Between all of these, gleaming cities stretched for miles and their metallic spires touched the crimson red sky.

Hovercraft like ships, a beautiful sleek design, streaked through the air, leaving behind a visible silver energy.

And just when they could see something else as well the image shifted.

A massive circular complex dominated the screen. Inside tall figures moved around. They were the same, purple coloured aliens with elongated features and piercing violet eyes. They looked just like Rirun and Oryx that Max had visualized. They stood over some glowing consoles, their hands moving swiftly over them as they worked on the alien technology. The tallest, looking like a leader, at least that could be assumed from the way he walked around with a completely different aura that he carried. He was draped in flowing metallic robes and then slowly turned towards the screen.

The air grew thick inside the Satian Hub, everyone fell silent as the alien's face became clearer.

There was a branding on his arm that was visible as he came near the screen and the members got a clearer view of him.

Veraux. The only thing they got was this and seemingly sounded more like the alien's name. But the question was why would the name be branded on his arm. Or was the branding meant for something else and not his name.

The alien stood in the heart of Tira Mira, the city they had just witnessed. His violet eyes gazed directly at them through the digital screen. His thin lips slowly curved into a smile that was more like a smirk as if telling them they cannot do anything now.

Max's breath caught in his throat and almost fell back looking at the alien up close. He could not balance himself and almost tripped over Brooks. "He sees us."

"Are you fine?" Brooks whispered in Max's ears.

"Yeah. It's just- I don't know actually. Was it because I saw the alien up close or was it something else, I don't know."

"You sure? Wanna get out for a few minutes?"

"No, that's fine, I'll be good. Let's concentrate on what this projection is telling us now."

"Fine, if you say so."

The screen flickered once again.

Veraux was even closer to them. It almost felt as if he would come out of the screen the next time. This was nothing less than a horror movie. Veraux tilted his head slightly and spoke in a low, commanding tone to another figure that was out of their view. The language was alien just like them, but something about their tone and expression was strangely familiar.

Veraux's gaze was fixed onto Max. It felt as if he could kill Max through his piercing gaze.

"Do they know about us?" Anarina asked.

The alien's lips moved but once again talking to someone else who could not be seen on the screen. But this time as he spoke the only problem was that he was completely inaudible. All they could do was understand his lip sync.

"We have been looking," was what Carrey interpreted, but they were not sure whether he actually spoke those words or something else.

"Wait a minute." Max suddenly said.

"What happened?" Stones asked.

"Does this mean all of this is not some vision, or the past. Does this mean that he is actually in front of us just separated through the digital screen?"

"Now that you actually said that you can be right. It makes complete sense. The way he stared at you, the way he tilted his head and the way he looked at us when he was talking to someone else. Why would this happen if this was not live?"

Veraux interrupted their talks and said with a smirk on his face, "So you guys finally realized that this is live and I am no vision that you are visualizing."

"What does this mean?" Max said out loud but sounded calm.

"It means what you just heard. This is no past or some vision that you are visualizing."

"What do you want from us?" Stones asked.

Veraux did not answer that but all he said left the others in anguish.

"What does he mean by saying 'we'll meet again.'?" Vela asked with confusion, anger and frustration written all over her face.

"Did we lose signal or did they do this on purpose?" Tim asked.

"They cut it. Definitely they did it." Max said with surety being filled in his tone.

The ground rumbled beneath them.

"Yeah. Great. What else have they left us to experience?" Lisa said sarcastically.

"I don't know what they want or what they are trying to do. But for now let's get out of here and find some solution. We need to contact UGSA again." Olivia suggested.

"Yeah, let's do that." Lisa sighed.

Just as Max was about to take a deep breath, he received a call. On checking the caller id, he was completely irritated, he almost wanted to throw away his handset. Finally picking up the call, Max turned pale as he couldn't believe what he heard from the other end. As minutes passed by he did not know how to react.

"What happened? Do you want to head back to the base camp?" Ean asked

"No, but the call was from the headquarters. And the news that I just got-" He could not even complete his sentence.

"Do you want some water?

"First sit down and take deep breaths. Stabilize yourself. And once you are fine, tell us what they told you." Hills suggested taking out a candy looking pill. "Hey have this, it will give you energy and calm you a little bit."

He did as Hills told him. After a few minutes, he was back to normal. He could breathe properly and felt slight relief spread over him. He started, "The activation of the Kabbot and the Satian Hub sent an invisible shockwave through the earth's surface. Every place is affected. At first it was just a guess but now it's sure that it is not just this island but the entire Earth that is affected. The activation has disrupted the electromagnetic fields, radio waves and what-not."

"Anything apart from that?" Tim asked.

"Yes there is more to it. In fact a lot more."

Everyone's faces grew pale.

"Thousands of satellites orbiting Earth wobbled, luckily this was only for a few minutes, but it can create a problem and a major one if it happens again. They went completely blank. GPS signals vanished and the space stations reported some mysterious magnetic anomalies disrupting their instruments. Seismic-"

Before he could continue, Ed interrupted him, "You said what, Mysterious magnetic anomalies?"

"Yeah, he said that. Now shut up and listen to him first, there is more to it." Jones said to him.

"Right, so what I was saying was that seismic activities across the globe spiked. The UGSA reported minor tremors that were felt in California, Japan and the Andes, and more shockingly all occurring at the same time. In a matter of a few minutes entire global communication networks failed. There was chaos all over and we did not or will not know if any of this happens again until the UGSA calls and tells us."

"Can't we just simply have some broadcast or report switched on, on our phones?" Ed suggested and after rethinking again said, "Never mind there may be no network for us to watch it live."

"Yeah and more than that, if the satellites had gone blank then it is definitely not possible for them to get to show anything live at least for the next half hour."

Stones said with a calm voice.

"Do you think it's extremely bad over there?" Rox asked hoping the answer would be a ....No though deep down she knew the truth.

"It is. In New York, Wall Street came to a screeching halt. Stock market screens flickered and glitched, sending out false data before it went blank. Traders who were used to commanding the world's economy stood helpless as the servers crashed and the transactions froze. A frantic financial analyst slammed his fist against his computer, 'we are one for real. Every network server is down and we cannot track any of the transactions.'"

"What else?" Brooks asked.

"The subway system failed leaving thousands of passengers stranded in total darkness. Emergency lights flickered and the people screamed and shouted. They could not ask for help since there was no signal, no internet or any sort of source available. In India where millions relied on cash, long lines formed outside banks but the ATM's were all useless. In London, air traffic control lost all connections to their flight crossing the Atlantic Ocean. Pilots flew the planes blindly without any sort of GPS or satellite guidance. In Shanghai, an entire district went dark. Skyscrapers stood silent and everything went blank. It felt as if the entire district was dead. Global shipping routes collapsed. Cargo ships struggled to continue with ports and automated tracking systems failed. In the Middle East oil refineries went offline causing a sudden spike in prices. In short, all over be it Paris, Tokyo, name any place the situation was the same. Either systems crashed down, electricity went out and traffic control was out of control as well.

"What the? How did this happen?" Juno said.

"You know the answer very well." Lisa said it casually.

"Yeah I know, but yet."

"Guys this is not the time to discuss who and how it was caused." Ean said. "Did the media react to any of this?"

"Of course, how can they not? Despite the satellite blackout, they managed to send a few snippets across social media. A few military radio frequencies were still functioning and were not impacted by the blackout, so they were used to broadcast the chaos. The anchors on all major news channels were completely shaken and it was so clearly visible. Netizens on social media called it a celestial event, government conspiracy, a doomsday and yet a lot more."

"Wow! The media doesn't leave one chance to cover any sort of news and the social media can never let a news not become a speculation or a rumour, does it?" Lisa said sarcastically.

"Even the United Nations Headquarters was held in darkness, the power grid had been rerouted to backup generators, barely enough to illuminate the room. But guess what even this was possible for just a few minutes and then boom it all went blank."

"Okay, yeah, this is more than just bad.?" Rox whispered.

"What do we do?" Emo asked.

"We have to come up with a solution. And that solution needs to be thought about quickly without wasting too much time." Olivia replied.

Chapter 9

El-Bon

"Let's look around the Caniula and the Calendula if we find something that would help us." Lisa suggested.

"I think that's a good idea." Rox replied.

They started their search around the Caniula, its stage and the entire amphi-theatre.

"I wonder if they held dramas and danced around this stage." Tim jokingly mentioned.

"Yeah, they did. This was actually the place for their entertainment and meetings also." Brooks replied.

"Wait, what? Are you serious?"

"Yeah, you thought I was joking, especially right now?"

"Umm, I guess yes but never mind I didn't know you were serious."

"I don't think there is anything. We've already seen all of this earlier." Carrey said.

"I guess we are just wasting time looking around here. Why don't we go inside the Satian Hub? We will get most of our answers there. And probably even the alien, what was his name again- Veraux, yeah, he might just tell us something." Ean suggested.

"Makes sense actually." Jen replied. "And another thing is we can divide ourselves into two teams. One goes to the Satian Hub and the other searches the Caniula and the Calendula."

"That's a really good idea. I think this makes a lot of sense and it would even save us time and effort." Stones agreed.

"Then let's divide ourselves into teams." Lisa said.

"Brooks, Olivia, Ean, Tim, Carrey, Vela, Hills, Jones and I will go to the Satin Hub and the rest will look around. If there is anything you'll find then immediately inform us." Max suggested.

"Got it." Stones reassured.

They headed towards the Calendula. On entering, everything seemed to go back to normal. They moved further towards the Satian Hub. The first step into the Satian Hub and the emergency lights flickered. This was the first time they experienced it, something that did not feel monotonous, but obviously not something that felt good as an experience. The broadcast shifted from a grainy video to a chilling clear one.

On the screen was a planet, a colossal binary star system burned in the sky, casting pretty hues of crimson blue and deep amber across the alien horizon. The planet's landscape was both familiar and bizarre, towering blue mountains, rivers of aqua coloured water and the dense forest of red leafed trees. The view they had already viewed earlier but this time it was not just there was a lot more to see.

"Woah, that's a whole city except for the fact that it looks a lot more advanced." Tim exclaimed.

Beyond the alien wilderness, metallic spires spiralled high. Suspended highways criss-crossed the air, where sleek car-like planes zipped and zapped through the sky like silver arrows. The civilization was highly advanced far more ahead than that of the Earth.

Ean scrambled to pull out his tablet, his fingers moving fast as he jotted down notes.

The aliens were purple, the shades differentiated the males from the females. The males had sharp cheekbones and grooved foreheads. Their thick unibrows and side-set, fish like eyes with glowing blue irises gave them almost predatory looks. Their hands were long and flexible. Their blood purplish blue due to cyanoglobin, glowing slightly when they were exposed. They wore sleek, metallic clothing adorned with jewelry that signified their ranks and achievements.

And suddenly the screen flickered. The beautiful landscape was replaced by a face.

The deep voice of Veraux rang through the Satian Hub and the digital conference screen.

"YOUR FUTURE IS IN OUR HANDS."

The words sent a chill through the room.

Max's heart pounded against his ribs

Lisa took a shaky step forward, "Oh my God... At first it all seemed just like a warning, who knew it was all true," the words came out almost in a whisper barely audible.

Vela's fingers trembled over the tablet she held, "It's a two-way conversation let us try once again asking what is going on."

The camera panned out, revealing a row of aliens who were disciplined standing behind Veraux, their gazes piercing and their expressions void of emotion.

A second screen flickered and within the view a new figure entered.

He was taller than Veraux, his fingers elegant and long adorned with metallic rings, his sharp facial structure carried an air of absolute authority. His shade of purple throughout the body was different from those of the others.

A title beneath his image appeared and was instantly translated by the Satian Hub's interface.

SYCON- SUPREME RULER OF EL-BON

"Who is he?" Jones asked "What is El-Bon?"

There was no response from anyone, all the eyes were glued to the screen as if waiting for a reply from the other side.

The moment Sycon spoke, the air grew even more thick. "You have opened the gates and invited this upon yourselves," his voice deeper than the ocean carrying no anger or malice, only certainty. He continued, "Inhabitants of Earth, we didn't actually think we would get to meet," he said with a grin on his face. His gaze was piercing and held a weight of a feeling of uneasiness as he glanced through every human present in the Satian Hub.

"But who are you?" Ean asked.

"Sycon, the leader of this planet, El-Bon," Veraux said, giving an introduction to their leader.

"Your species has stumbled upon forces beyond your understanding, and now we have re-established contact with

Earth, thanks to you," said Sycon.

Max asked, "What do you want from us?"

"Earth," the only word that came out of Sycon's mouth.

"You said what?" Olivia almost blurted out.

"Yes, Earth. Obey our command and you will be rewarded. Surrender to us or face extermination."

He leaned forward towards the camera, giving them a clearer view of his facial features.

"No, that is not possible."

"Of course it is. And you will make it possible for us" Sycon and Veraux laughed.

"But why? And why do you wish to take over the Earth?"

"You are our resource and we have the means to acquire that," said Sycon."

"Let's have a mutual agreement where both the parties will be at a benefit. Doesn't that sound better?" asked Max, not quite understanding what Sycon meant by "You are our resource".

"Negotiation is for equals, compliance is for unequals," thundered Sycon.

"We have advanced capabilities to counter your threat," spoke Max.

"So what is your high point?," questioned Sycon.

"We are nuclear capable and can thwart any invasion, replied Max."

"Oh that's primitive for us, we are Quantum, so no point in trying retaliation or resistance."

Ean, still frantically took notes of it all.

"Why can't we discuss PEACE," quipped Brooks.

"PEACE COMES AT A PRICE," retorted Sycon.

"Look, we are explorers and scientists. We mean no harm to any of you and do not wish to disrupt your peace. We will immediately leave this island if you tell us."

"Petty humans," Sycon uttered angrily and instructed Veraux to continue conversation with Max and get the leadership of Earth online. After instructing, Sycon left the scene.

Veraux leaned forward slightly, his dark purple skin illuminated by the flickering glow. "So dear explorers get your leadership to talk to us before that window of opportunity closes on you and we take your planet hostage."

A slight murmur left Carrey's lips, "We are a fragmented civilization without any global leader."

Veraux slowly exhaled. "That makes my job easier, because divided you not only fail but also fall."

"I shouldn't have installed the Kabbot," cried Max, realizing and revealing the truth behind the alien voice cautioning them to do so,

Hearing this, Veraux laughed.

"So you talk about "Rirun-the traitor." He backstabbed Oryx, our former leader of El-Bon and Rirun was the main cause for our losing control and contact of Earth."

Nobody could grasp what Veraux was implying and why Rirun was the alien traitor and defector.

More questions than answers, all playing out in front of them without any idea where all this was heading to.

Veraux's fish-like eyes studied him for a full minute. Then, he smiled, though it was anything but a smile of warmth.

"There is no way you can get out of this, you have to comply with our orders."

The realization hit them hard. The implication was clear, this was not a warning but a calculated certainty.

Max swallowed hard. His fingers hovered over the control panel, debating whether to shut down the system. But something within him told him not to since it wouldn't stop the alien from harming them.

Tim came forward, "We are not here to cause you a threat. We don't intend to interfere with your world."

Veraux's unibrow arched slightly, "That could have worked, but you carry our important resource which is essential for us," grinned Veraux to the disbelief and dismay of all.

"What do you mean?" Max furrowed his brow.

The screen flickered and the image of Veraux momentarily disappeared. The image that was visible was now swapped with that of dead bodies.

"What...what is this?" Vela asked.

Veraux's image returned, "These are the dead bodies of aliens and humans who went against El-Bon. They defied certain rules and instructions given to them and this was the result of their disobedience. The same goes for you guys if you do not do what is told to you."

Everyone fell silent and the Satian Hub suddenly felt cold. They also remembered the skull rocks which they had earlier seen and the human remains during the trek.

Max was completely dumbfounded and had no idea of what to say. His fingers trembled as he gripped for some support.

"Tell me, are you ready to pay the price or listen to what we are telling you to do?" Veraux asked with a smirk on his face.

Brooks took a step forward, "What exactly happened to those?" he asked, pointing to the image on the screen.

"Oh them, they wanted to cause rebellion and defied what was told to them. They opened these doors for themselves, just like you'll have opened these doors for yourselves."

"So you are saying all of this is your doing?" Ean asked.

Veraux let out a low hum, "Not mine. Theirs." He gestured towards those on the screen who were now lying lifeless.

A heavy weight settled over the group as they exchanged worried glances towards each other. They could not decipher whether it was a warning or a threat.

"We have to consider the possibility that whatever happened to them could... could happen to us as well." Olivia said.

"But what was it that led them to such destruction?" Ean asked curiously.

Veraux's lips curled in a smile,

"Some truths are not to be revealed."

Max exhaled, "So what do you want us to do, he asked Veraux."

"Get your act together and connect us to your leadership and await further orders," ordered Veraux.

Suddenly the screen went blank and the hub was in the middle of a deafening silence.

"Why does he suddenly disappear?" Brooks let out a sigh of frustration.

"Forget his disappearance and re-appearance, what is necessary is what we saw just now on the screen." Max suggested.

"That's actually true. We need to really think about it. What does it all mean and what he meant to tell us? What could have led to all the happenings to those dead aliens and humans?" Ean added.

The screen was back to life once again, but this time instead of Veraux or Sycon, it was the civilisation of El-Bon.

"Wait, did he really have to do that and give us a clear reminder of what will happen if we won't comply with what he says."

Next a map of El-Bon was visible.

They all leaned in. The planet's surface was a detailed one, sprawling cities, vast oceans, dense red-leaved forests and many unfamiliar landscapes. A series of glowing symbols dotted in different regions and shockingly each one pulsating faintly.

"Are they some sort of markers?" Olivia pointed out.

Ean's tablet once again switched on as he made notes of it. "Probably some sort of important location, who knows."

"Do you think they would be of some importance to us?" Brooks asked.

"Probably, wouldn't that be the only reason for the image to appear." Max answered.

"Or maybe to distract us. I mean it's just a possibility." Brooks added.

"Can be. Do you think we can zoom this in and get around the marker to know what it is?"

"You wish you said that probably even a second back." Ean said while keeping his tablet aside.

Max turned around to only see the blank screen.

"Are you serious? Why does he even do this if he does not want us to get close to any clues?" Max let out a frustrated cry.

"It's fine, right now we need to think of a way to save the Earth from these aliens and also keep in mind the fact that they have their eyes on us." Olivia suggested.

"I have an idea." Tim spoke after the Satian Hub fell in a deadly silence. "We can connect with the UGSA–"

"How do you think they are going to help us?" Max didn't even let Tim complete.

"Let him finish what he was going to say." Jones stepped in before a heated argument would arise.

"Yeah. Sorry. I didn't mean to interrupt you but-"

"It's fine. Don't apologize. I know you are under a lot of pressure coming from the UGSA and the current situation we are in."

"Yeah, but anyways you continue, What's your idea?"

"So what I was saying is that we get out of here and connect with the UGSA. We can get them to find out more about El-Bon, by sending them data that we have gathered on this island, if that's possible. Through that we will be able to get a little idea about what exactly is the planet made of and what are those secrets that they are trying to hide from us."

"I don't think they would help us."

"Why do you think so? We haven't even given it a try." Olivia said, agreeing to Tim's idea.

"Yeah, and what's the worst that could happen?"Brooks asked.

"Fine then let's give it a try but I just gave you'll a heads up beforehand, so if it does not work out, no one can blame me. "Done." Tim said optimistically.

They got out of the Calendula. Everyone gathered around the centre of the Caniula and the entire event was explained to the rest of them. They were also informed of the decision that was taken at that moment.

All of them retreated back to the base camp. None had the energy to speak anything except Ed who really wanted to lighten up the mood but every effort he made went in vain.

They reached the base camp and the first thing that Max did was to contact UGSA. Tim stood right beside Max to hear their conversation.

At first Max was hesitant but then finally dialed the headquarters.

"Have you come up with a solution already?" The person on the other end asked.

"Umm. Not exactly, but we need your help to hopefully get a full proof solution."

"What can we do for you?"

"There is this planet called El-Bon, we are sending you all the information and data that we have gathered on this island about this planet. We want you to search and find out more about this Planet & share that information with us. Whatever is possible from your end. Is that possible?"

"Sure, we will try our best to get you some information regarding that. What was the name of the planet again?"

"El-Bon." He repeated.

"Noted. Give me sometime I'll get back to you as soon as I get some information."

With that the call disconnected. Right after that, Max did not dare to look at Tim out of embarrassment.

"It's fine you don't need to feel embarrassed about it." Tim said as if he could read Max's mind.

"How do you know, I was actually thinking or feeling that?"

"I think there is something known as brotherly love, I guess it's just that."

Tim made a great attempt to crack that joke and it hit exactly at the point making both of them fall in a fit of laughter.

"What's all this laugh about?" Anarina asked as she brought back with her two cups of coffee for Max and Tim.

"Just something that stays between both of us." Tim looked back at Max and once again tried too hard not to start another round of laughter.

"Weird, anyways, had a word with UGSA?" Anarina asked.

"Oh yes, let's gather everyone, they might call back anytime." Max replied.

"Everyone get back here." Tim shouted which almost felt inaudible in the chaos.

No one paid attention and as a matter of fact his voice was not even audible in the activities everyone had busied themselves in.

"Did they just ignore me?" Tim commented with a look of that of a small boy with an innocent face that could melt anyone.

"Probably, no one was interested in listening to you." Anarina laughed.

Max tried hard not to laugh on Tim's face, "Anyways we have gotten something known as walkie-talkie's to connect with people and if not that then we've even gotten legs to run over and call others." Max gave a sarcastic comment.

"Sure. You may now keep your mouth shut and call others and tell them that UGSA has agreed to help us." Tim smirked.

Max forced a smile.

"Are you both done taunting each other, can we call others?" Anarina asked before they would go on and about teasing each other.

"Of course." Max said as he removed his walkie-talkie.

At the same time Tim ran over to call Carrey and others who were towards the waters.

They all gathered around the breakfast table and the latest update was given to them. They waited for the call from UGSA to think about their next steps.

After a few hours that felt like almost forever, Max's handset rang. "It's from UGSA."

"Of course we know that, receive it, will you."

Tim once again commented.

“Have patience, I am doing it.”

“Can you both just keep quiet, you both have been like this for the past half hour.” Anarina said, frustrated.

Both of them just gave each other a look and then finally Max received the incoming call.

“Any news about El-Bon?” Max asked, keeping aside all the greetings.

“Yeah. In fact, quite a bit of information, processed from the data gathered from the island as submitted by your teams and further deep space observations carried out by UGSA, it’s just I am not sure how much of it will be useful for you.”

“That’s fine, we will figure that out.”

“The planet is nestled within the unmapped TQX44B1 galaxy. It orbits the larger of the two stars in a binary star system. It is the fourth planet in its system, roughly about the size of Earth, but the rotation period is 20-hours, splitting its day and night in an equal 10 hour cycle. However, due to the presence of two suns, it never sees darkness, only a soft twilight when the smaller star dips below the horizon. One revolution is 300 days. Its axis is tilted at 27 degrees and has a gravity of 9.1 The sky of El-Bon is unlike anything seen in the known universe. During the day, the crimson blue atmosphere stretches endlessly painted with wisps of silver clouds that shimmer as they reflect the dual sunlight. When the second star sets, the sky transitions into a deep violet haze, casting an ethereal glow over the entire landscape. The presence of multiple moons causes double eclipses, where both solar and lunar eclipses occur at the same time which creates a breathtaking celestial phenomena." The person on the other end paused for a moment.

"Are you describing El-Bon or some painting?" Max asked as he just could not believe the description given to them.

"El-Bon. Even we could not believe it at first. But this is the planet that we are talking about at the moment and it is no less than a beautiful mesmerizing picture kept in a showcase of an art gallery."

"Is there more?"

"Yes. The terrain is a striking contrast of familiar and alien elements. Towering blue mountains rise in the distance, their peaks crowned with frost that glows faintly under the stars. The oceans a surreal shade of aqua, their surfaces rippling with gentle waves that glisten under the binary suns. El-Bon's forest is something that truly sets it apart. Instead of the lush greens, the planet has a plant life of deep, rich red, creating an almost otherworldly contrast against the landscape. Some trees have spiral-shaped trunks, their roots glowing faintly in soil while others grow in twisting, arc-like formations. The fauna consists of six legged creatures, floating organisms that drift on unseen currents and predatory beings with shifting skin tones that allow them to blend seamlessly into the alien foliage. Their architecture is particular beyond human knowledge. They have flying cars zip effortlessly through invisible transit lanes. Structures built from holographic materials and translucent metals gleam under the sunlight, shifting in colour as they react with environmental changes."

"Please tell me this is all the appreciation that you can make of El-Bon. I really can't bear to hear anymore." Ed spoke.

"This is it at least for now. This planet is something else. It is teeming with life, both natural and engineered, a place where mystery as well as futuristic technology coexists."

"I know. We probably will find some clues through this. Thank you for your help and if you find something new then please inform us." Max said before ending the call.

"Damn. The description of this planet only tells us that there is something unique about it." Juno exclaimed.

"Did you guys notice one thing throughout the entire conversation?" Stones asked.

"What, exactly, are you talking about?" Lisa questioned.

"There are similarities between that planet and this island."

"What do you mean?" Ean asked.

"The bioluminescent flora and fauna that we have noticed here as well. It matched with the description that we got from UGSA as well."

"Yeah, that almost went unnoticed." Max replied.

"Why don't we look for some more clues that would give us some information relating to El-Bon. I mean we anyways have a pretty good description about the planet. So we might find something related or something that could bring us to some solution." Vela suggested.

"That's actually a good idea. We anyways have some time before we take some action so might as well use it like this." Olivia agreed.

"Let us all look around and make notes of it and in two hours meet here again and discuss it." Max said.

"Also let us all be in groups and not go around individually." Lisa warned.

"Yeah. Make teams and let us gather in two hours."

Everyone in groups of three and four scattered around the island. They went towards the water, caves, and forests and observed every detail they came across and made notes of it.

After about two hours everyone started retreating back towards the base camp where they were going to meet.

The last group came in and everyone settled in their seats with their observations close to them.

"Who's going first?" Lisa asked.

"I'll go." Jen answered. "The sky that was described to us and the sky that we see here during the time of sunset are pretty similar. Crimson blue skies that we actually don't see in other places as well."

"Oh yeah. How could we miss something like this-" Ed stopped momentarily.

"Something we actually see everyday?" Jen tried to complete his statement.

"Yeah."

"This happens because we have the tendency to not pay attention to something that we see almost everyday or have a habit of ignoring it since we see it everyday." Carrey explained the logic behind it.

"The water sources here. They are of aqua colour just like that of El-Bon. The lakes in the forest resemble the same colour." Anarina said.

"One of the main observations, the magnetic anomalies. The Satian Hub as well as the instruments malfunctioning near the seven pillars all prove this point." Tim pointed out.

For the next hour, while the sun was setting, they all discussed their observations and how they could not notice all these even if they were right in front of their eyes.

After an informative session all of them decided to go back to the Calendula to find something if they missed out, especially after getting to know about El-Bon.

Chapter 10

Tira Mira

The alien city of planet El-Bon, called Tira Mira shimmered beautifully under a lavender painted sky. Its mushroom shaped buildings cast elongated shadows across the translucent winding highways. Car planes floated through those invisible lanes, their undersides glowing as they raced their way. Bioluminescent flora spiraled along the sides of the buildings.

Alien citizens moved gracefully, some glided on single elongated limbs while others had wings or hovered on anti-gravity discs. Their conversations were sung in tonal pulses, resonating through the air in harmonic layers.

Glowing, spiral-shaped transport tubes zipped through the air, and below, large pools of semi-liquid material reflected the overhead structures with eerie precision. Floating gardens spiraled upward like green tornadoes, tended by drones shaped like luminescent jellyfish. Every structure appeared alive, organically grown rather than constructed, with surfaces that breathed and expanded slowly like lungs.

Among these surreal forms rose the largest of the towers, a majestic mushroom with a glassy dome at its top and thick, spiralling stems coiled across the base. Inside the nerve centre of El-Bon pulsed- the Unified Command Centre. It was elegant and fearsome, a mixture of polished alien engineering and natural architecture seamlessly blended.

Within the UCC, Veraux sat at the helm of a semi-circular command deck, his tall frame draped in a robe that seemed to ripple like liquid obsidian. His eyes unblinking, focusing on the three hovering holographic screens before him. Each screen hummed with kinetic energy, displaying vastly different realities at once. On the far left, a rotating hologram of planet Earth spun gently, its blue hue vivid amidst a field of data streams. The middle screen flickered with a celestial event: twin eclipses—one solar, one lunar—aligning over El-Bon in a rare astronomical dance. And on the rightmost screen, a view of the Calendula base on Earth played out, with its human operators frozen in a moment of curiosity, completely unaware they were being watched.

Behind Veraux, the command deck buzzed with controlled chaos. Uniformed alien personnel moved like clockwork, their elongated limbs gliding over floating control consoles, communicating in quick bursts of coded alien tongue. A quiet celebration was underway—muted, but unmistakable. Smiles curled on inhuman faces, soft murmurs of satisfaction passed between officers.

★★

The members, as pre-decided, left the base camp early in the morning and made their way to the Satian Hub. One thing was for sure that they would definitely find some clue from there. They just had to keep their eyes open and minds clear to view it.

The Satian Hub seemed the same as before, nothing about it had changed. They entered the Hub and the feeling of being watched over crept in.

They noticed that the Satian Hub was not shut down.

"Wasn't the Hub and the screens switched off when we left yesterday?" Brooks asked, skeptical.

"I am pretty sure it was." Ean replied.

"Yes. It was switched off. Probably it might have been Veraux." Max answered though he himself was not satisfied with the answer he gave. "Anyways let's see what the screen looks like and what it is ready to show us."

They neared the screen. They could not understand what was going on.

On the massive central screen within the Satian Hub, the alien city of 'Tira Mira' flickered into view. They could see everything, the moving walkways, the car planes, the shimmering towers. And then it zoomed in, pushing through the shell of a giant mushroom structure. The UCC unfolded before them in crystalline clarity.

"Woah! What is this structure?" Jen exclaimed. "It looks beautiful I suppose."

"It does, but at the same time it definitely has a lot of secrets hidden within it." Brooks replied.

"The question really lies, whether this is live or recorded." Vela asked.

It was all a blur. There was Veraux, the screens and the celebration.

"It seems more like a pre-recorded vision to me. Look at them celebrating there." Max said.

"But we don't know what they are celebrating." Stones argued.

"And why would they want us to see them celebrate?" Anarina questioned.

"If that's the case then probably even Veraux might not be knowing that the Satian Hub is showing us a vision like this."

The glowing screen flickered with light, drawing the attention of every eye in the room. The city of Tira Mira had faded from view and was replaced by the interior of the Unified Command Centre. Veraux sat there but this time, he appeared a little more composed and involved on the three screens before him.

The visual of the UCC was breathtaking and instinctively attracted everyone towards it. Its main deck was built within the hollow dome of a massive mushroom-shaped structure. The ceiling glowed with soft blue veins of light that pulsed in harmony with the station's energy core, hidden deep beneath the surface. Circular walkways spiralled around a vast central console, where rows of translucent pancakes floated midair, operated with mere gestures of the alien team. Their fingers danced in a deliberate movement over the controls, each action producing a ripple of glowing symbols in the air.

The walls shimmered with a pearlescent sheen, reflecting the multicoloured lights from a dozen of data streams. Hovering pods moved silently from one station to another, delivering devices or retrieving data cores. A soft hum filled the air, layered with the distant whirring of analytical engines and the low hum of the beamer—an enormous, ringed transmitter embedded at the core of the command deck.

Veraux appeared focused, issuing commands with a tone that radiated quiet authority. His face, though stern, carried the faintest edge of satisfaction. Around him his team worked diligently, their skin tones shifting slightly with emotion, an El-Bonian trait that was never noticed earlier by the team in the Satian Hub.

Max pointed to the screen, "They have always been monitoring the Calendula, look."

"But isn't this live? Those on the screen are the members from our team itself." Jen spoke with a tone of confusion.

"No, it can be recorded as well. They might have recorded our movements when we might have been discovering the Calendula." Ean replied.

"Then why does it feel like it's happening now?"

"It might just be an unsettling feeling that you have. You're probably overthinking it."

Just when Jen was going to say something, Olivia spoke with a tone filled with pure shock and surprise, "Everyone look at that... that looks completely unreal."

All the heads were towards the screen where Olivia had been pointing. Their faces held an expression of awe. They never in their wildest dreams imagined to view a double eclipse that too a lunar and solar, both at the same time. Something that is impossible to occur, is happening right in front of their eyes.

The golden sun, usually steady and warm in the sky, began to dim as the planet's smaller moon, pale and glass like, crept across its surface. The first eclipse took shape, a solar eclipse, a ring of bright gold flared around the silhouette of the moon, casting long sharp shadows across the alien cities and the mushroom towers.

At the same time, from the opposite side of the sky, the larger moon, dusky red, rose slowly, entering El-Bon's shadow. It too began to darken, slipping into a lunar eclipse even as the smaller moon covered the sun. The entire view was surreal. One moon was blocking the sun while the other was being blocked by the planet itself.

The sky dimmed into an unnatural twilight. The clouds turned violet. The stars began to show faintly, even though it was still daytime. The overlapping eclipses twisted the light into spiralling halos. Rivers shimmered with dual reflections. Bioluminescent plants were glowing bright.

Inside the Satian Hub, the entire team was motionless. They could not decipher what they had just witnessed. The strange alignment looked as though it was almost recorded and then edited to give such an effect. They could not take their eyes off of the double eclipse. It was just something that could not be put to words. The entire Satian Hub fell silent. They enjoyed a complete two minutes of a beautiful visual.

It felt peaceful, until they heard Veraux's voice.

"They really had to ruin the peace we received after so much we have been through, didn't they?" Jones said, frustration evident in his voice.

The members saw the screen witnessing the double eclipse being minimized and a screen that had Sycon online being maximized to almost full view. Sycon emerged from Culmina, a sprawling mushroom-like palace on El-Bon. Sycon's voice filled the command centre.

"Veraux." was the only word they understood. The rest was completely alien to them.

"Can't they talk in a language that even us normal humans can understand?" Max let out his frustration.

"No, they aren't talking to us. This is supposedly between them and something we shouldn't be knowing." Stones replied. "Anarina, can you translate what they are saying?"

"Sure thing."

Anarina laid out all her equipment and set the entire thing up. Everyone intently watched her as she unpacked her stuff and laid out everything and linked it to the Kabbot and the other devices.

"I wonder the last time when we were here, the Kabbot translated the content for us, but why isn't it doing it today." Brooks questioned.

"Probably if the Satian Hub is activated by the aliens then the Kabbot also activates and works as it is supposed to. I mean I can be wrong but for now this is what I can think of." Stones replied.

"That actually makes sense." Lisa agreed to what Stones said.

While everyone was watching the entire system being set up, Tim and Jones were busy discussing something else.

"Okay, done setting up all the required equipment. Now I just have to connect it to the screen and the Kabbot," Anarina said.

"Great. How much time would that take?" Max asked.

"Just a minute." Anarina replied. "Good to go. Everyone, this is now connected and we will be able to hear what they are talking about."

"Guys, Tim and Jones listen to what they have to say or you'll argue later." Lisa said, her voice loud though a little calm.

Everyone fell silent and were carefully listening to what Veraux and Sycon were saying.

"We have acquired Earth's coordinates. The alignment is occurring now and the signal is steady." Veraux reported.

"Proceed with preparations." Sycon commanded.

"What preparations are they talking about?" Tim asked out of curiosity.

"Shhh. If we listen we'll know." Jones told him.

"You will dispatch the Elfa to Earth," commanded Sycon.

"You wish to send the Elfa right now?"

"Yes." Sycon said. "Debaush will lead."

A murmur rippled through the UCC as officers began initialising commands.

"Debaush. Sounds like a warning bell." Carrey remarked.

"Do you yet think this is the past?" Jen asked once again.

"I don't know actually. Maybe it is or maybe it isn't. But if it isn't in the past then we are in a horrible situation, more like in the middle of a war." Max replied.

"They literally sound like launching a mission. If this was the past, it would have already occurred but this has still not taken place." Jen spoke, frustration evident in her tone.

"But they probably never launched." Max argued back.

"Guys, stop arguing with each other, probably Jen is right. If we listen to their conversation we will get to know if it's the past or the present." Anarina spoke to avoid the heated discussion.

"Get Debaush online," Sycon's deep voice caused silence among the members in the Satian Hub.

Debaush was briefed about the mission by Sycon before giving final clearances to Veraux for lift off.

"It...It is in the present." Max said it out aloud, his face turning pale. "What are they planning to do to Earth?"

"We have to do something about it." Ean said.

"Let's first call UGSA and inform them." Brooks suggested.

Before they could take a step ahead, they saw the Elfa getting ready for the launch. The spaceship was enormous and out of the ordinary. A completely different look from what they had seen in movies and drawings.

The Elfa rested within a dimly lit hangar deep beneath Tira Mira, surrounded by a circular platform lined with golden rings. The sheer size and design of the star ship brought to fore the technological prowess the alien civilization had achieved. With no visible seams, outer skin shimmered like a liquid metal, changing its colours from dark violet to silver constantly reacting to the energy coursing its structure. Delicate etchings ran along the sides of the ship, symbols in the El-Bonian language that pulsed faintly under the shifting angles of the light. Wings extended slightly from the ship's flanks, thin and curved panels. The ship had three decks: Upper one presumably command deck; middle one, the admin deck; and the lower one, system deck. The cockpit was barely visible from the outside. From the inside, a pilot would see in all directions through a panoramic neural display. There were displays and controls in the centre of the command deck. The ship flew by using quantum energy.

Everyone stood in awe of the space ship. The look of it left everyone speechless.

Just when they were admiring the beauty of the Elfa, they saw an alien come into view.

"Is that Debaush?" Ed asked.

"Debaush is ready and waiting for the signal." Veraux announced.

The Kabbot in the Satian Hub pulsed faintly. The team felt something, a feeling of something going wrong.

Just as Debaush entered the Elfa, the spaceship lit up. But surprisingly he was yet waiting inside and did not begin with whatever their mission was.

Inside the Unified Command Center, Veraux's focus remained locked on the console before him. The beamer's resonance deepened, and streams of alien glyphs moved across the UCC's outer display wall. Several command officers stood at attention behind him, waiting for the final order.

On Veraux's main display, the final set of launch pre-checks came online. The Space ship ELFA was ready to launch.

Veraux stood silent in the middle of the command platform. All around him, systems remained in standby. Elfa was ready. The crew had done their part. Only Sycon's final word remained.

Yet the screen that once displayed the ruler's towering figure stayed blank, its frame outlined faintly with dormant energy.

"Why hasn't he replied?" one officer asked quietly.

Veraux didn't answer. His gaze remained on the still image of Earth.

"Are they still waiting for something? I mean, doesn't the spaceship look completely ready to be sent?" Ean remarked.

"Probably they are waiting for some other order or they are just doing this on purpose." Vela said undoubtedly.

Veraux remained motionless, seated at the helm. His silver purple eyes flicked between his command interface and the hologram of Earth, hovering just above him. The silence from Sycon lingered like a shadow, stretching too long.

"Pilot Uck is requesting authorization," came a translated voice from Elfa's internal comms. "Flight path locked. Dimensional pulse charged. Awaiting mark."

Veraux leaned forward slightly. His fingers hovered over the interface. But he didn't touch it.

He stared at Debaush's image, jaw tightening ever so slightly.

And then, came the go ahead. Sycon authorized the mission for lift off.

A huge plume was seen as the Elfa lifted and in a split second vanished from sight.

Veraux moved slightly towards the screen that displayed the Calendula. His eyes grew narrower and his gaze even more sharper.

"Can he see us?" Stones questioned.

"I think so. He can probably feel the link, now that the Kabbot is slightly pulsing." Anarina replied.

"He hasn't spoken to us yet, which can be an assumption that he hasn't even seen us." Ean tried to justify the other possibility.

"If he gets to know we are watching them then there could be danger for everyone, in fact the entire earth." Olivia warned.

"But what can we do anyways?" Jen asked. "It's not like we can shut it down."

"We can, can't we?" Ed replied.

"Absolutely not. This can turn out so bad if something goes wrong." Lisa looked at Ed.

Veraux turned towards another alien, at the controls.

"Keep me updated on the mission," Veraux commanded.

"Yes sir," replied the alien.

Suddenly, the main feed glitched. Just for a blink, but enough. For one frame, the image on their screen showed themselves.

The Satian Hub. The team. Looking into the screen.

Everyone's face turned pale. They did not know how to react and what to tell Veraux if he discovered the fact that they heard the entire conversation.

And then it flicked back to Veraux, who was now actively monitoring the flight path of Elfa.

Anarina stepped away from the console slowly. "He saw us."

Brooks didn't move. "Just a flash. Maybe not enough to process."

Max turned to Anarina. "But enough to feel."

Back in the UCC, Veraux briefed Sycon about the progress of the mission.

He said that Elfa could reach Earth soon and minute by minute updates were being transmitted from the Elfa to the UCC.

Chapter 11

Elfa in-charge

The Satian Hub's display still buzzed with residual light from the final live transmission. The alien city of Tira Mira had vanished from the screen and Veraux's piercing gaze was the last image they viewed before it had all disappeared.

For a moment, no one moved.

After a minute or so, even the residual light was gone. The entire system was now pitch black, every display, every interface had gone dead.

Anarina stepped forward slowly, as if drawn by some magnetic force. The once glowing glyphs had faded, leaving behind only the quiet hum of an invisible presence.

"They are planning to attack Earth." Anarina said, her voice filled with fear.

"That's not possible." Max rejected the thought.

"Then why would they send the Elfa to earth?"

"I don't know, but what would they get by attacking the earth anyways."

"They have their own motives, Max. Think about it."

"How do you know what they are planning to do?"

"I just read the alien glyphs before it all switched off."

"I think you are just overthinking it. Even if they think of doing that it would take them more than100 years for Elfa to reach Earth." Max joked and shrugged the situation.

Amidst their conversation, Tim stepped in and announced that his instruments once again started to malfunction.

"Let me try and connect with the UGSA headquarters." Max said.

He dialed the first number on his contact list but it didn't go through.

'Connection failed.'

He tried once again but the result was the same.

"I can't get them on line, did they cut the connection?" Max asked bewildered.

"Didn't I tell you that they are planning to attack." Anarina said, her tone a little harsher than she expected.

"Can we try and re-establish the connection?" Lisa asked.

"Trying. Wait a minute, it is in progress." Tim answered.

Ed and Vela ran up from the Satian Hub to the Caniula to find some network or even if they could work through transmitting electro-magnetic waves. Ed's voice crackled through the radio, "This is Ed...."

"We cannot hear you." Brooks announced through the other radio they had.

Since neither of them heard each other, Ed and Vela ran down back to the Satian Hub. "Seems like the radios are also not working. The connection is completely destroyed, be it within the island or even outside the island."

Max kept on trying to get in contact with the UGSA but every try just led him to failure. And just when he was about to give up, he received an incoming call. "Unidentified number." He announced.

"Pick it up." Rox called out.

"Hi, this is Kash from the GUF." His voice was not clear but they paid complete attention to what he had to say. "We have gotten all the information related to the ongoing situation from the UGSA. But we need the latest update from you guys to think about the next step."

"GUF?" questioned Emo.

"Global United Forum, established immediately consisting of expert disaster and crisis management teams from across the world to address the developing situation, headed by me." Kash answered.

"So as of now, we saw that Veraux with the commands from Sycon has launched Elfa with Debaush in charge of it." Max informed and then the call ended.

Like the cold breath of a machine exhaling its final command, the last glyphs blinked on the central console: 'Q-Maze: Live. Initiated. Lockdown Complete.'

Anarina stared in disbelief at the message and was brought back to reality after a few nudges from Lisa. "What happened?"

"We are in trouble."

"What do you mean?" Max asked with a look of concern and curiosity.

★★

Within the hour, the repercussions of the Satian Hub's silence rippled across the planet Earth.

The first to witness it came from Chile. "We've lost all telemetry. Every geosynchronous satellite is dark. It's not space debris or solar activity. Something's interfering with the network. Something... deliberate."

Then came the cascade.

From Singapore's aviation towers to Frankfurt's trading floors, Tokyo's subway network and New York's emergency systems, everything depending on satellite communication began to stutter. Lights flickered. GPS signals turned erratic. Commercial airlines hovered mid-air, unable to coordinate with air traffic control. Trains slowed, then halted completely. Financial tickers froze, their last movements mid-crash.

"It's happening again and I don't think this is going to be lenient like the last time," she said flatly. "System by system, node by node. They're shutting down the scaffolding of modern civilization."

Lisa looked up from a backup console, grim. "That's not just a satellite blackout. That's strategic deactivation. They're hitting infrastructure."

Tim chimed in, sweat streaking his forehead. "Orbital scans are impossible. Telescope data is static. The space above us is quiet. Too quiet."

From the emergency ham radio positioned in the corner, a familiar voice crackled through.

"This is UGSA Emergency Ops. Confirm: Is this the ICMR team? Please respond. Earth's satellite grid is collapsing. We've lost ninety percent coverage. We are attempting contact with global stations. All lines are unstable. Do you copy?"

Max rushed to the receiver. "This is Max. We confirm interference began after last contact with Satian Hub. Q-Maze appears activated. Earth is being gridlocked. Repeat, gridlocked."

The line crackled.

"Understood. We have reports of global system failure. Civil aviation is grounded. Military command lines... unstable. Do not panic. Await further instruction."

Then, static.

"Gone," Max muttered. "They're gone."

The entire team, scientists, explorers and even the linguists weren't prepared for this global warfare and shutdown. Almost all of them stood blankly staring at the dead screens and unresponsive instruments.

Anarina looked at Max, more like a stare that would pierce through his soul, "Didn't you say this would at least take a century?"

"I was wrong." Max apologised.

★ ★

Across the world, chaos had ignited.

Beijing, China:

Air traffic towers were plunged into darkness. Dozens of passenger planes turned back. Red emergency beacons flashed on the ground as thousands of citizens gathered in confusion, their phones suddenly useless.

Berlin, Germany:

Traffic systems collapsed. Massive pileups occurred across the autobahns. Sirens blared then fell silent. Military convoys scrambled, headlights cutting through streets now dim and uncertain.

São Paulo, Brazil:

Live news anchors screamed into dead mics. Emergency networks tried routing messages through landlines. Cell towers blinked off one by one.

New Delhi, India:

The power grid flickered, then blacked out. The metro halted underground. Passengers wept in darkness.

New York, USA:

Stock exchanges collapsed. All indices froze mid-crash. Citizens rushed to banks but transaction systems failed. ATMs dispensed blank receipts.

Cape Town, South Africa:

Radio DJs tried to calm the city through analog transmission. One final message made it out before the towers failed: "Stay calm. Something is happening. The world... the world is changing—"

Everywhere military generals and other leaders leaned over the dead screens. Military strategists stared at the projection wall. It displayed a map with a growing red zone spreading across all continents. Diplomats screamed in ten languages. Reporters stared at the cameras that no longer could broadcast anything. Citizens gathered in the thousands in city squares, looking skyward. Children clung to their parents, pointing up at a sky where no planes passed and no drones buzzed. Entire neighborhoods shut down as electricity blinked off like dominoes falling in the dark. In the distance, churches, temples, mosques, and shrines rang bells, blew horns, or sang prayers in an age-old attempt to reach the heavens.

★★

Back at the Satian Hub, the Kabbot pulsed again. The surface that had once faded into silence, now shimmered with a static, chaotic energy spread across and the colours violently ran across its grooves.

Tim stepped back, eyes wide. "It's reactivating..."

Anarina was already moving toward the center panel. "No. It's responding."

Max stood frozen. "To what?"

A sudden thunk echoed from the console. The center display flared blinding white.

Across the world wherever emergency power still flickered screens came alive.

The same image materialized in millions of places at once: a wide control deck aboard an alien vessel. Towering spires in the background. Panels lined with strange biomorphic symbols. And at the center, seated on a throne-like metallic dais, a figure with glowing cyan blood threading beneath dark purple skin.

Debaush, his face elongated and alien, but intelligent and expressive filled the screen.

Max took a step forward. "That's Debaush."

Scene at GUF Headquarters: Geneva.

A sudden beeping alert brought the attention of every global leader in the room.

Screens across the conference lit up simultaneously.

"Is this a hack?" Kash spoke, his voice loud.

"No, sir," a technician answered, voice trembling. "We're not receiving... we're being transmitted to."

Debaush leaned forward, eyes scanning, almost lazily. The lines on his neck pulsed with glowing blue. When he spoke, it was in perfectly translatable Earth dialect, his voice smooth, deep, and chilling.

"Greetings, citizens of Earth. I am Debaush, appointed chief presiding officer of Elfa. Under the command of Supreme Leader Sycon of El-Bon. Your communication channels now belong to us."

He raised a hand. Behind him, an alien interface flickered into view, a three-dimensional projection showing Earth's orbital sphere surrounded by thousands of tiny moving points.

Anarina's eyes widened. "Those are our satellites... They're mapping them in real time."

"As you've likely noticed," Debaush continued, "Your sky no longer obeys your will. Your machines no longer listen. Your words no longer fly. You are unplugged."

Back at the Satian Hub, the display adjusted, splitting into three. One panel showed Debaush. Another showed the outer shell of Elfa, gliding silently, orbiting above Jupiter's magnetic veil. The third showed Earth itself.

"Sycon," Debaush announced, "Has declared Earth a dormant civilization. Unworthy of autonomous control. Henceforth, all planetary command will be directed by the Ascendancy of El-Bon. You will not resist. You will not defy. You will bear allegiance."

Then came the words that made the blood of every human listener run cold: "YOUR FUTURE IS IN OUR HANDS."

Anarina gasped, stepping back. Her mind echoed with the memory of the first pillar. The one none of them had fully deciphered. The one she had read under her lens, days earlier, 'Your future is in your hands.'

The contradiction screamed in her mind. She clutched the side panel, whispering, "It's... it's a hijacked prophecy. They twisted it."

At the GUF headquarters, Kash stood, eyes wide in disbelief. "What the hell does that mean?"

Back on the island, Max felt every fiber in his body tighten.

"This changes everything," he muttered.

Suddenly, Debaush's voice boomed again, more urgent this time responding to something unseen off-screen: "Prepare for the next phase. Lock Phase 2. The grid must not fail. All activities must be geared towards the final purpose of Elum Extraction," he told UCK, his second in command.

Tim turned to Max. "Did he just say 'Elum'?"

Max shook his head. "Yeah, but what does that even mean?"

Lisa leaned over the screen. "I think we're about to find out."

The screen shimmered violently, signal distortions cut through the alien transmission and then, as suddenly as it began, everything went black again.

Total silence returned.

Max slowly exhaled. "They're preparing something bigger."

Anarina closed her eyes. "And we stand no chance."

Somehow Kash got into contact with Max and confirmed whether all of what Debaush said is real or not.

"It is all real." Max replied. "They've activated a full orbital lockdown – Quantum Maze. Every satellite under Earth's control is now compromised. I think they've deliberately left a few connections and pathways open for us."

Kash questioned, "Is this all from the device that you activated with the Kabbot?"

"Yes." Max did not deny. "It was a trigger and it was not all our doing."

"Where is the Elfa? asked Kash."

"The last signal came from beyond Jupiter's magnetosphere. But the technology they use is extremely advanced to let them hack our entire infrastructure and control it the way they want to, Max explained."

"Can we neutralize the source or something?"
questioned Kash.

"No. Destroying or neutralizing cannot be done as we do not have the technology. Moreover, Elfa is not here. Their command centre is also not here, neutralizing it wouldn't impact them at all. They have already hacked our systems. They've left these few systems open for us is all a part of their plan. We probably have no take on this, it is what they say we have to do," replied Max.

"It could even make the situation worse if we try to do something that would retaliate against their system and have repercussions on us." Anarina added.

A faint hum buzzed another frequency trying to breach. And the screen switched without warning.

Once again on the screen was Debaush. "Greetings, again my dear citizens of earth. We welcome your attempts of rebellion and we admire your spirit as well but hear this loud and clear, you can resist and delay but your fate is written by us now and it remains unchanged."

★★

Back at every other place on the earth, every minute there were new changes that the people got to witness. The first time was fun to view since it was something new, but now, all it created was fear.

In the Northern Hemisphere, Auroras erupted across skies where they shouldn't be, swirling crimson and violet and dancing in the magnetosphere.

In India, families poured on their terraces. Children pointing at the sky which was now a dull grey. Streetlights flickered and then dimmed completely as electromagnetic interference spread like a veil.

There were gravitational anomalies detected in Canada. At first they were minimal and later as minutes passed by it kept on expanding.

In Africa, nomadic tribes gathered in clusters, watching as the sky above them was split. A sandstorm began unnaturally, swirling not from the wind but from some other external forces.

It was not just the mountains and the skies and the waters that viewed these crises but even the flora and fauna were deeply affected by those. Their behaviour was not fine. Whales and dolphins in the oceans started abruptly circling in panicked patterns and the plants and trees bent in an unnatural form.

★★

On the island everything seemed to pause. The glow from the plants and animals had dimmed and the waves seemed to pause. They could hear the whispers of the pillars from far off. The island's central lake shimmered with unnatural light. Its surface now pulsed with slow, concentric circles. The same rings from Elfa. The same glyphs from the Kabbot appeared just beneath the water. Everything seemed to go beyond their natural properties.

Max looked around everything. His eyes glanced at all the tired and pale faces around him. He could not help but feel sorry. His face a reflection of clear regret wishing he hadn't taken such a bold step without weighing its consequences. He did not have the courage to say anything to anyone. But at the same time he knew that this wasn't the time to feel sorry and cry over something that was already done, knowing fully well that Struggle & Challenges are wired in the DNA of

LIFE - No ESCAPE! He quickly changed his demeanor and convinced himself no matter what he will do his best and not give in.

They returned to the base camp. Their heads could not take in anymore of such information at that very moment. They needed to rest and make themselves calm. Their minds, swirling with the overload of information.

As soon as they returned back to the base camp, they faced a backlash from the GUF and UGSA.

Chapter 12

Q-Maze

Kash, stood before a massive multi-screen control deck now flickering, now static. He had witnessed wars and diplomatic breakdowns, but never this, a total, simultaneous blackout across every technologically equipped nation.

"Get me Max," Kash screamed, frustration clearly audible. "Now!"

The operators scrambled with analog phones, bouncing signals across patchy lines. In less than five minutes, a heavily distorted image of Max flashed onto the screen.

"Max, you've got some explaining to do," Kash said coldly.

Max's face was a mixture of disbelief and guilt.

"We didn't anticipate this," Max said. "It's not the Kabbot. It's... it's something else. The Satian Hub activated something we couldn't predict."

Kash didn't blink. "You're telling me we handed over Earth's operating system to a freaking glowing cabbage." Kash could not control his anger anymore looking at the current situation in every part of the globe.

"It's a multidimensional transmitter, not just an artifact!" Max snapped back. "It connected to something... bigger."

"No, Max. You're explaining it. Now."

In the room behind Kash, global leaders gathered, some in military regalia, some in traditional robes, others in solemn silence. From presidents and country heads to leaders of all hues, the collective gaze bore down on Max.

Suddenly, Olivia appeared on Max's side, gently pushing him aside. "We need to go back to the hub. The answers are still there," she said.

In a corner, Carrey, the psychologist scribbled frantically in her notebook, her fingers trembling. "Human response patterns to existential threats... unknown. Emotional saturation... maxed." Her voice barely registered over the room's turmoil.

Tim, behind Olivia, adjusted a portable scope. "There's a repeating pulse in the air, the frequency matches the insignia patterns we've seen. The quantum field might be embedded in the island itself."

"Then we go," Max said, his voice hardening. "I'll assemble the team."

Kash's eyes narrowed. "You've got one chance, Max. If this doesn't fix it, every sovereign nation on Earth will decide what to do next. Including eliminating that island."

Max swallowed hard.

The screen cut to black.

Back on the island, the wind rustled through broken ferns

and alien bones. Five figures assembled silently near the Satian Hub's crumbled archway. Max, Olivia, Tim, Anarina, and Emo, carrying their gear, prepared to re-enter the heart of the storm.

The island groaned beneath them, whispering secrets no one yet understood.

The walk back to the Satian Hub was tense with unsaid words, crackling with an energy only partially explained by science. Thick mist rolled over the alien vegetation. Each footstep crunched on glistening foliage that glowed faintly, as if bioluminescent. Every now and then, the wind carried a mechanical buzz, a tremor in the earth, as though the island itself was alive and watching.

"Did you see how Kash stared through me?" Max muttered to Olivia. "He wasn't just asking for answers. He was judging humanity's survival by what I said."

Olivia adjusted her pack, eyes focused on the path. "That's because the whole planet is leaning on one decision, ours. And if we mess up again, we're not getting another shot."

Anarina, walking slightly ahead, paused as a soft humming returned to her ears. She turned her head slightly. "It's the same frequency from the pillars," she murmured. "I think the entire island's network is active. Like it's pulsing with intent."

Emo trailed behind, lens in hand, murmuring to herself. "If the Q-Maze is activated remotely from Elfa, maybe this place is a node... a relay. Maybe there's a second layer we're missing."

"Tim?" Max called over his shoulder.

Tim checked his readings. "Electromagnetic interference is back. Compass readings are in reverse again. It's like we're heading into the heart of a black mirror."

They descended. Anarina walked directly to the Kabbot and without hesitation, pressed both buttons, one glowing softly, the other pulsing blue.

The Satian Hub screen flared to life.

Debaush's face appeared immediately, as if he had been waiting for them.

"Ah," he hissed in near-perfect English, though laced with a grainy accent. "As expected."

Max stepped forward. "Why are you doing this? Why Earth?"

Debaush smiled, revealing jagged silver teeth. Behind him, alien officers manipulated translucent control panels. "Because Earth contains precious resources for us and humans are those resources."

Anarina clenched her fists. "You've hijacked our world, taken control of every form of communication. What's the endgame?"

"DESTINY GIVES CHOICES, PERISH OR PREVAIL, PROGRESS OR FAIL, pronounced Debaush."

"The Q-Maze," Debaush said. "Earth is now within it. The maze cannot be exited unless Sycon commands it. All your satellites, networks, and frequencies are governed now by us."

Max's heart pounded. "You've turned Earth into a puppet."

"No," Debaush replied coldly. "We've made Earth obedient."

The transmission glitched, momentarily showing a backdrop of celestial bodies, stars, a burning ring, and a blue sphere unmistakably resembling Earth. Coordinates flashed in alien script.

Emo's eyes widened. "Did anyone else see that?"

"Yes," Tim whispered. "They're closer than we think."

Back at GUF headquarters, Kash watched the live stream with jaws clenched. The other leaders gasped as the alien message echoed around the war room.

Elfa stationed near Jupiter was visible on the screens.

Anarina stood silent. Then she said, "We need to listen to the pillars again. They may have the answer. And there is a possibility we might have misheard 'Know-where to see.' as 'No where to see.'"

Night on the island didn't feel like night anymore. The sky remained a strange hue of aquamarine, pulsating faintly. Though Earth was supposedly cut off, the Satian Hub still buzzed quietly connected to something beyond, something unrelenting.

Inside the Hub, the team sat in silence around the pedestal where the Kabbot glowed intermittently like a heartbeat. The air was heavy with electromagnetic pressure. Tim took out his portable scanner, muttering, "Even without a satellite relay, the Kabbot is emitting directional pulses—narrow beam transmissions, possibly quantum encoded."

"What does that mean for us?" Emo asked, pushing her glasses back up her nose.

"That we may not be alone even now," Tim said. "The pulses... they're being answered."

Max stood at the console, staring at the image of Debaush still fresh in his mind. "We need more than answers.

We need leverage."

Anarina stepped away from the console and walked towards the semi-formed concentric circles surrounding the Kabbot pedestal. She bent down, studying the carvings. "They're not just decorative. They're linguistic. A primitive syntax, but definitely a map. Look closely every third curve aligns with the groove inside the Kabbot."

Olivia leaned in. "Could this be the map Emo was talking about?"

"Yes," Anarina whispered. "But it's encoded in symbols of events, not coordinates. It's a sequential history carved into stone. A timeline."

Tim snapped his fingers. "Wait! That would explain the reverse readings! If the Kabbot is relaying echoes from the past to inform the present, then these grooves are time-encoded paths. The map isn't spatial, it's temporal."

Emo's eyes lit up. "So each activation doesn't just show a scene, it shows a fragment of Earth's fate through the eyes of whoever touches it?"

"Yes," Anarina nodded, her voice suddenly sharp. "But only if you know where to touch."

Suddenly, the ground shivered beneath them. Olivia staggered back. "Was that an earthquake?"

Max steadied himself against the wall. "No. That felt like a burst of energy."

In the distance, they heard a low howl, metallic and mournful. It echoed through the basin.

"Something else is waking," Tim murmured.

The storm inside the Satian Hub wasn't made of clouds or lightning. It was made of uncertainty, whispers, and pulsing lights. As Anarina carefully brushed away dust from the time-map, Max stood with Olivia, their voices low and taut with tension.

"They've hijacked our present," Olivia whispered, watching the slow pulse of the Kabbot. "But are they using echoes of the past to do it? If we can trace the echo backwards..."

Max finished her thought, "we find the source."

Before anyone could respond, the Kabbot's pedestal emitted a deep harmonic tone. Then the display screen came alive without a prompt, Debaush again. His face filled the screen with unsettling calm.

"Still trying to resist?" he asked. Behind him, the command center of Elfa buzzed with controlled chaos and aliens rushing between consoles, monitoring Earth's activity.

"This ends now," Max said, stepping forward. "You've made your point."

Debaush leaned closer into the screen, his eyes glowing faintly. "No, Max. You still think this is a negotiation. It is not. Sycon has already declared himself the ruler of your world."

"You're trespassing," Olivia snapped. "This is an act of war."

"We don't war," Debaush replied. "We redesign. Your fragmented governance."

Anarina's voice cut in sharply. "And yet you fear the Kabbot. Otherwise, you wouldn't monitor every interaction we have with it."

Debaush's smile faltered for a moment. Then the screen blinked and shifted to a wide view of the Elfa's deck. They saw alien officers engaged in strange, coordinated gestures over glowing panels. In the background, through the transparent hull, Jupiter loomed large. Debaush's ship was closer to Earth than anyone had realized.

"You will comply," Debaush said finally. "Or Sycon will declare total dissolution of your regimes. And we will take what we want."

The screen faded to black.

Max stood frozen. Olivia gripped his arm. "They're bluffing. They have to be bluffing."

But Max's silence said otherwise.

Back at the GUF headquarters, chaos surged. The live stream had reached every emergency communications network on Earth. Kash slammed his fist onto the round table. "They're positioning to take us. Our satellites are gone. Communications compromised. We are officially... isolated."

A young analyst ran into the chamber. "Sir, observatories confirm Elfa's trajectory. They are stationed at the Lagrange point near Jupiter. Cloaked... but visible now. Our scopes just aligned."

Murmurs erupted among the gathered leaders grappling to come to terms with the developing situation around the world.

Kash turned slowly. "Then it's real."

Inside the Satian Hub, the team stared at the now-black display screen. Anarina's fingers were tracing the grooves on the floor around the pedestal, her mind miles away, decoding fragments not only in language but in energy.

Tim was running recalibrated scans. "There's a fluctuation every time someone repeats one of those phrases like the Kabbot responding to resonance, not just touch."

Max exhaled sharply. "So it's not just tactile input. It's voice. Frequency. Intention."

"Yes," Anarina said slowly. "It's more alive than we thought. It's choosing how much to show. And to whom."

Back at GUF headquarters, chaos had metastasized into grim silence. World leaders stood around the circular table, the emergency red lighting casting everyone in shades of war.

Kash paced slowly. "They're creating something around us. We can't see it yet, but it's closing. It's a cage."

An intelligence officer rushed in, panic evident in her voice. "Sir, global GPS systems have lost their navigational coordinates. We've lost temporal synchronization across multiple sectors."

Another chimed in. "Time on Earth isn't syncing with UTC anymore. The clocks are off. By seconds. But growing."

Kash froze mid-step. "They're bending time?"

"Or remapping it," the officer replied grimly.

In a corner, an ambassador from Brazil whispered to another, "They're invading us and they're rewriting the rules."

Another leader quipped, "We wanted to go in search of aliens but they found us."

No one moved within the Satian Hub, it fell completely silent.

A new image flickered on the screen: Debaush, again but this time from inside the GUF headquarters. Everyone gasped.

"No, no, no, that's impossible," Max said. "How is he there?"

But Debaush wasn't there physically. He was digitally projected onto the main wall at GUF, hacking into the communication network, his voice magnified through every broadcast channel Earth had left.

He was smiling.

"People of Earth," Debaush began, his tone almost theatrical. "You have seen glimpses. Hints. But now, I will bring you clarity."

Kash stood stunned as the projection continued. The faces of global leaders around him twisted in disbelief, who were still trying to understand what is happening with the world.

"Sycon has declared himself as the rightful custodian of your timeline. Your systems, your skies, your choices, all belong now to us. You are in the Q-Maze, and the maze is alive."

On hearing this, one leader blurted out, "Let's finish the aliens who cause us harm".

"To resist," Debaush said, "Is to dissolve. To align... is to survive."

"Give us what we want and we give you what you need," he added. "Soon Sycon will address the world, stay tuned."

The screen blinked off.

A deep hum began emanating from the Kabbot again lower this time, more urgent.

Outside the hub, the storm grew bigger. Red and indigo bolts snaked across the sky, charging the air with static that made every breath electrified. The Kabbot's hum deepened to a low, trembling frequency. The grooves around the pedestal began vibrating in rythm.

Tim placed a copper coil against the floor. The needle in his device began spinning wildly. "This is reaching outward, calling something or warning something."

Suddenly, the display screen flickered. This time, it wasn't Debaush or a memory. It was real-time, a live feed from GUF headquarters.

Kash stood at the front, expression grim. Behind him, the war room was darker than before. The backup generators were all they had.

"Max," Kash said, his voice rough, "They've shut down every remaining channel. Only this line remains and even that, we don't control. Debaush hijacked it again."

He paused. "He just issued an ultimatum. Total surrender or Earth's neural grid will be reset. Globally. Our entire memory infrastructure... wiped."

A long silence followed.

Then Kash added, "People are panicking. But they're also waiting for you."

Max stared at the screen, his heart pounding. "What do they expect us to do?"

Kash didn't blink. "Give us a reason to believe we're still in charge of our destiny."

The feed cut. The silence in the Hub was louder than a scream.

"I don't know if we can deliver that," Olivia said quietly. "We're chasing whispers while they control the skies."

"No," Anarina said firmly, stepping toward the Kabbot. "We're chasing truths. And maybe... they're buried deeper than we thought."

"Let's start from the beginning, especially the whispers we heard from the pillars." Olivia suggested.

★★

Back on earth everything halted, it all went to pre-industrialization. Airports abandoned, control towers dark, hospitals almost non-functional except routine check-ups that were possible, trains immobilized, internet gone, markets collapsed and people communicating through letters, megaphones and hand signals.

In New York, skyscrapers stood as dead monuments. Elevators froze mid-flight. Office workers were seen opening sealed emergency stairwells with crowbars. Paper signs replaced digital screens.

In Tokyo, battery-powered radios relayed a single emergency frequency repeating: "All citizens remain calm. National signal outage confirmed. Communications under review." Streets once glowing with LED signs were lit only by lanterns, candles, and car headlights.

Bicycles and rickshaws replaced cars.

In Berlin, clock towers were manually reset by watchmakers. Generators powered by diesel and coal were dragged from basements and retrofitted. Mechanics worked on hand-pulled carts to move food between towns.

All security systems were down, and no war machines were working. Also missiles were no longer firing.

Military jets sat grounded. Air traffic control towers flickered with static. Currency systems collapsed as bank records were lost, people bartered with food, medicine, and warmth.

The world woke up to a new reality and everything was happening in such quick succession that there was barely any time for anyone to respond.

Anything and everything that was human creation with the help of technology had come down. The internet, a tool that had unified the world, was gone. The Earth had, in a single day, returned to the era of steam, fire, and paper.

Minute by minute, hour by hour the crisis only deepened.

★★

Meanwhile, the explorers, scientists and the others were all trying to find the answers buried deep within the island.

Anarina crouched with a weathered journal and several rubbings from the stone. She traced the markings on the pillars once again.

Olivia sat beside her, hair tied in a bandana and skin tanned from the weeks of fieldwork. "Still working with the same thing?"

Anarina did not answer that question. She carefully brushed the dust and then whispered, "We were wrong."

"About what?" Olivia asked curiously.

"The inscription on the pillar says "YOUR FUTURE IS IN YOUR HANDS" whereas the alien says "YOUR FUTURE IS IN OUR HANDS." Anarina wondered if there could be a connection between the two.

"How did we not get that? And now that we think about it, it makes sense also. How could we miss such a simple detail." Olivia said, frustrated.

Just when Olivia was done getting frustrated over the small mistake, Emo whispered, "We missed one more detail."

"What is that?" Anarina asked.

"I just decoded the whisper we were trying to decode for a long time. It is 'Go there to see.' It probably did carry some importance but if only we could decode it earlier we would have probably caused a little less harm to the entire globe." Emo answered.

"How many things did we miss and also misunderstand?" Jones said as he heard their conversation from behind. Small things make big difference.

On the other hand, Vela could not stop herself from rethinking all the decisions she had made in the past few weeks. Also a thought lingered in her mind, "How could the broken part of the kabbot land in the sea? And how was it cut?" She sat on a low sitting in the Caniula, staring at her fingers and letting her tears flow free.

Ed, from behind, put his arm around Vela's shoulder to comfort her. "You okay?"

"I shouldn't have gotten that Kabbot from the shop. I should've known that behind its beauty lay something even more dangerous."

"It was indeed beautiful but none of this is completely your mistake. Don't blame yourself for something you did not do."

"But I was the one who bought it even on this island. If I would've left it back at home, it probably wouldn't have caused all this damage. I could feel it pulsing but I ignored it thinking it was my imagination but I was wrong. It was all a means to re-establish this entire system. And I am the culprit who has gotten everyone in this trouble."

"No, stop overthinking it. It is not your mistake. Everyone is in this together. No doubt that after bringing the Kabbot here, we have faced several issues but at the same time we found what we came here for. We explored the island and not just that but also discovered various things that not anyone even knew about. So stop thinking about it. It is not your fault whatsoever."

"But-" Ed did not let her complete her sentence and spoke, "We didn't start this Vela. We were just the means to get this entire system back to life. Now let's go back, they are all waiting for us."

Ed comforted Vela but deep down, he himself was feeling guilty for getting both the lost pieces together and combining the entire piece.

Unfortunately it was not just the two of them who felt guilty, deep down each and every member present on that island felt guilty and wished it was just a bad dream and that it would end soon. All of them held their feelings strong and controlled themselves so as to not demotivate others with them.

At the end of the day, all of them gathered at the base camp and anxiously awaited further orders from GUF.

A team from GUF was now stationed at the Satian Hub to monitor the situation closely.

★★

THE AFTER MATH: Humanity in crisis

The sudden turn of events rocked the very core of global equilibrium. What began as an obscure scientific expedition had escalated into a planet-wide alert. Earth could no longer afford to remain a silent observer.

As if awakened by an existential threat, all nations of the world responded in unison. No longer fractured by borders and ideologies, expert teams and reinforcements were mobilized from every continent to the infamous island—once hidden from the world, now the eye of the storm.

The island was no longer just a forgotten landmass, it had become the epicenter of frenzied activity. Scientists scrambled to decode energy patterns. Diplomats whispered of war. Generals sharpened contingency plans. The very soil of the island seemed to pulse in rhythm with the global heartbeat.

Talk of a final, desperate solution emerged: obliteration. Destroy the island, neutralize the threat. The idea gained traction, especially among those watching their world unravel. But caution prevailed—leaders hesitated, wary of igniting something they did not understand.

Then came the ultimate display of human defiance. A missile, manually launched from a state-of-the-art warship, streaked across the sky with lethal intent. But the response was swift. The missile didn't explode, in fact, it didn't even land. As it neared the island, it simply... stopped.

The world watched, dumbstruck, as it hung mid-air, stripped of momentum. Then, slowly, it crumpled inwards and dropped into the sea with the grace of a feather. No sound. No fire. Just silence.

It was the shield. A tri-layer quantum defense system that shimmered invisibly above the island. The first layer seized the missile, halting it instantly. The second disarmed its warhead. The third expelled it, leaving it as harmless debris swallowed by the ocean. Many more missiles fired at the island met the same fate.

The military might of all major powers was in full display in the vicinity of the island. A sight never seen before in the history of Earth, but to no avail.

The world watched closely as major powers grappled with the situation helplessly and all attempts turned futile. Lasers fired were also deflected by the quantum shield.

And then, every screen on Earth flickered.

From televisions in living rooms to the vast digital billboards of Times Square, from smartphones in pockets to high-security government monitors, all of them changed.

A sigil appeared. A swirl of geometrical light, rotating slowly, pulsing with an eerie cadence. Then came the voice. Smooth. Unfathomably calm.

"Greetings from Debaush."

The message played across all channels simultaneously, translated perfectly into every language known to mankind.

"Sycon, the new leader of planet Earth, will now address you."

The screen transitioned. A towering chamber came into view, angular, impossibly large, lit with floating orbs of liquid light. The camera panned to the center, revealing an alien being unlike any the world had ever imagined.

SYCON.

He radiated grace, terror, and intelligence in one impossible fusion. Behind Sycon, through translucent glass, the stars shifted in a dance foreign to Earth's sky.

"Dear humans," Sycon began, his voice a blend of choir and machine, a whisper that resonated in the chest more than in the ear. "This is Sycon from El-Bon."

As you are aware, your planet Earth is in the Quantum-Maze, through which we control all your activities and thereby your Destiny....Within this lattice, all your actions, intentions, and outcomes are regulated.

The image behind Sycon shifted. A cosmic map unfolded, galaxies branching like neurons, stars blinking like eyes.

"We watched as you launched weapons and as you debated our destruction."

"Any uprising, rebellion, or retaliation will be seen as acts of violation and will be dealt with effectively."

"You shall take orders from Debaush who is in command and will show the way forward."

"Your co-operation with us will be the PRICE OF YOUR FREEDOM."

"You can make the process PAINFUL or PAINLESS."

"THE CHOICE IS YOURS."

The screen shimmered. Then darkness.

One final phrase appeared, etched across the globe's collective vision.

"THE BEGINNING"

Soon after, chaos descends on Earth and massive protests break out in different parts of the World.

"Down with Sycon," "Down with Aliens,""We Want FREEDOM."

In the sequel

With Sycon of El-Bon seizing control through the Quantum-Maze, the fabric of reality itself has changed.

But the story is far from over.

In the sequel we'll explore:

Why does Sycon want to colonize Earth?

Is it for conquest, or something far more profound?

What next for human civilization?

Can societies adapt, or will resistance rise from the ashes of submission?

Is it the end of the human race?

Or is it the beginning of the end of Sycon?

Who are the enigmatic aliens Oynm and Suryl?

What roles did they play in Earth's forgotten past—and its unfolding future?

Was Rirun an alien traitor... or Earth's silent savior?

How did he sabotage the plans of Oryx, the architect of El-Bon's dominion?

What do the mysterious markings mean?

The insignias carved into the Pillars of Oynm, the crystal encasements of Suryl, and the circuits of the Quantum Resonator may hold the ultimate key.

And finally... Can Earth be freed? Is there a way out of the Quantum-Maze? And if so—who will reveal it? When? How?

The answers lie hidden... in time, memory, and the final confrontation that will decide the fate of not just Earth, but the very nature of free will in the universe.